Sc

Also by John Yount

*Wolf at the Door*
*The Trapper's Last Shot*
*Hardcastle*
*Thief of Dreams*

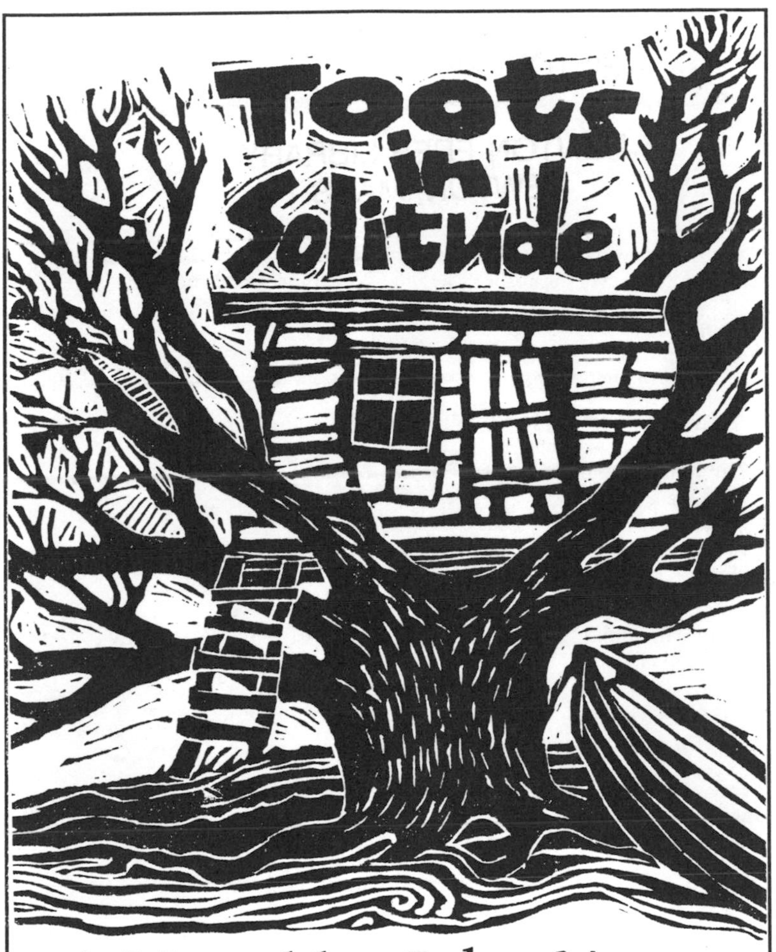


# A Novel by John Yount

Southern Methodist University Press
*Dallas*

This novel is a work of fiction. Names, characters, places, and incidents are either the product of the author's imagination or are used fictitiously.


First Southern Methodist University Press edition, 1995

Requests for permission to reproduce material from this work should be sent to:
Rights and Permissions
Southern Methodist University Press
SMU Box 415
Dallas, Texas 75275

**Library of Congress Cataloging-in-Publication Data**

Yount, John, 1935–
Toots in solitude : a novel / John Yount. — 1st Southern Methodist University Press ed.
p. cm.
ISBN 0-87074-384-8 (alk. paper)
I. Title.
PS3575.089T6 1995
813'.54—dc20 94-43858

*Cover art and design by* Barbara Whitehead

Printed in the United States of America on acid-free paper
10 9 8 7 6 5 4 3 2 1

For Jenny and Sarah

# I

An hour and a half earlier, in total darkness, the crowing of roosters had raked the dreams of the sleeping and shouted down all the lesser choruses of the night, until, when the roosters ceased at last, every creature was subdued and hushed, and the night was mute and black as ether between the stars. But now the eastern horizon had begun to pale so that the river and the alluvial fields of stock corn to the east and the wooded bluffs to the west were beginning to assume shape and proportion, if not yet color. Increasingly, birds made small remarks from places unseen, and the river began to throw off its coverlet of fog.

A raccoon bumbled along the eastern shore, rump higher than his withers, looking for one last crayfish or wounded minnow, until, through the varnished odor of the river, he caught a whiff of man, lifted his bandit's head, and paused a moment. Twenty feet from shore a wooden johnboat dallied slowly at the end of a rope. A third of a cinder block tied to the other end had been flung over a willow, which, like many others along the shore, leaned out over the river, dripping its leaves into the smoking water. The raccoon puzzled, bumbled on a few feet, stopped and tested the wind again, but, able to divine neither the threat of danger nor the promise of food, went on while the johnboat sawed gently in the current.

The body of a man lay on the bottom of the boat in two inches of bilge water, his hands folded over his chest in a perfect parody of death were it not that his feet, in high-top black tennis shoes, were crossed at the ankles as well, and the damp tendrils of his mustache stirred slightly with deep, even breaths. He had a full beard; hair to his shoulders; and a vicious, if long since healed, wound across his face that had taken a divot of bone from his temple and the bridge of his nose, as well as the eye in between. He wore a Band-Aid over his empty eye socket that snuggled nicely in the runnels where the outside edge of his eye socket and the bridge of his nose ought to have been. The remaining bottom two-thirds of his nose was aquiline, somehow even more like the beak of an eagle than it otherwise might have been, and somehow, peculiarly dignified. Perhaps because there weren't many mosquitoes, perhaps because lying in the cold bilge had cooled his flesh so much they had trouble finding him, only a few were drinking his blood, most of them arranged on the knuckles of his hands, two on his face; but they bothered him not at all.

Thirty feet or so up the bank a barred owl swooped at the raccoon and popped her bill menacingly as she passed over his head, but he was accustomed to such attentions, although usually only when he had been eating eggs or nestlings and usually from smaller antagonists. She wheeled and dived and popped her bill at him again and again until he was a satisfactory distance from the tree hollow where her downy owlets jostled, tipped like drunkards, and blinked at one another. The man lying in the bottom of the boat didn't stir at the ruckus she made, and even the raccoon seemed largely to ignore her except to put a stubborn bow in his back as he ambled on up the riverbank.

Downstream something better than a mile, two early fishermen backed their boat trailer into the water, and the faint confabulation of their directions to each other, the car doors slamming, a paddle clattering against the duckboards of the boat, and at last the guttural snarl of their outboard engine—all these sounds—traveled up the surface of the river as though it were a telephone wire. Sometime later, chased by the silver vee of their wake, they passed the johnboat. They saw it tethered in its odd spot but not its owner asleep in the bottom. Still, neither the din of their passing, nor the later undulations of their wake, caused the sleeping man to stir. Indeed the sun was well up and the birds were feeding in the mulberry tree arching high over his head before he roused. Even then it was a mulberry, pecked and rejected, hitting him square in the middle of the forehead, that popped his blue eye open. It was the only movement he made, but it seemed violent, fierce, and alert, at least for the few seconds he stared straight up at the dappled, bird-fluttered tree. But then he groaned, and blinked, and his blue eye turned mild as a cornflower. He tried to rise and found himself all but paralyzed with stiffness and pain, and so, lay still again as though considering the bleak aspect of resurrection. At last he began to search his pockets with swollen-knuckled, mosquito-bitten hands until he found and withdrew a few damp bills and some change. Except for a split-bottomed chair with its legs cut off just below the rungs, there were no seats in the boat; nevertheless, he seemed to know it was behind him and blindly pawed the air in back of his head with his fist of money until he found the seat of the chair, released the damp bills and coins, and let his arm fall again across his chest. He sighed, gathered resolution, and rolled over the side of the johnboat into the river like a turtle slipping off a log. The boat was so broad-beamed and heavy it scarcely tipped, and for nearly a minute after, the man's groans rose in bubbles to the surface.

# 2

Even after the river had loosened his stiff joints and sore muscles and altogether washed away the itch of his mosquito bites, Macon "Toots" Henslee hung on the side of the johnboat and lay back, trying to recollect just how he had come to spend the night in his boat. He'd sold his fish at Hobb's and sat down to have a few beers, but then had gone off to the rodeo at the fairgrounds because Duncan, one of the worst old sots at Hobb's, had worked up a fixation on the subject. Duncan had his wife's car and meant to drive out to the rodeo, even though he could scarcely navigate from his bar stool to the rest room. Toots remembered that three or four of them, having failed to argue Duncan out of his notion, had gone along to make sure Duncan didn't drive, or otherwise get himself into some godawful trouble. But Duncan had gotten under the steering wheel in spite of them and somehow managed not to wreck or get picked up, although everyone in the car was giving him advice, directions, cursing him for a fool, and even snatching at the keys in the ignition. Toots remembered all that pretty clearly despite the little alcohol-burning motor in the center of his brain that had started up even before he'd left Hobb's, purring away, muzzy, warm, and ridiculously content with any circumstance. After he'd gotten to the fairground and bought a pint of corn whiskey from an unlikely pipsqueak of a boy in a pickup truck, the evening got a little disconnected in his memory. He recalled snatches of bronco riding, calf roping, and the practiced Texas twang of the announcer over the loudspeakers. He recollected a Brahman bull somehow getting out of the temporary, hastily thrown-up stock pens and trotting about the parking lot among cars and pickup trucks, causing kids to spill their cold drinks and popcorn, men to laugh and hoot, and women to scream. He remembered the alert, fierce look of the beast, how much lighter and quicker it seemed to be on its feet than the cutting ponies the cowboys rode, but he didn't remember it seriously charging anyone, or even how the matter was ever resolved. And he remembered Louise, his former wife. He hadn't seen her in half a dozen years, but that hadn't kept her from telling him what a bastard he was; how he had ruined her second marriage by making her a joke and a laughingstock to her second husband, whom he hadn't even met for Christ's sake; and on and on.

What he didn't recollect was how he'd ever come to be in Louise's company. Had he spoken to her? He doubted it, but who could tell what sort of silly thing a fellow might do when he'd had a little to drink and was out to have a good time? If he'd spoken to her first, he was certain he'd been pleasant. He was nothing if not a pleasant son of a bitch. But he suspected she had merely seen him among the crowd and swarmed him like a hive of bees. Had she been drinking too? He wasn't sure how much she might have changed in all the years since they'd been married. Naw, hell, Louise was never one to take a drink. She didn't have to; she could get more unreasonable than any drunk just by catching a whiff of alcohol close to her. God forbid she should ever drink it. Did he recall her threatening him with the boyfriend she'd had in tow? He had a vision of a big, meaty-faced fellow wearing a leisure suit and a befuddled, wry grin; had a vague memory of the two of them exchanging pleasantries while she harangued them both. Like the business with the bull, he had no firm memory of how the encounter had ended; but, except for the affliction of sleeping in his boat and that deceitful little motor in his head that could purr while he was drinking and then seize up with such pain while he slept, he had suffered no damage, so Louise probably hadn't been able to sic her beau. How he'd gotten back to Riverside

Drive, however, mystified him. Some good soul had driven him, but he had no memory of it. Obviously he'd been able to get in his boat and start home and, no doubt, decided to stop and take a little nap along the way. Oh well, he thought, another little piece of his life mislaid; it wasn't as though he was the sort of fellow who had to keep strict account.

He lay in the water, his beard bouyant, his hair floating in a fan about his shoulders, wanting to feel good, wanting to feel he was doing all right; and, a little at a time, a comfortable sense of his freedom, his possibilities, his relative youth came to him like conjured spirits, a bit amorphous, a little worn, but with no apparent sense of their own ridiculousness. Macon "Toots" Henslee couldn't really quite fathom his age, which was a few weeks short of forty-nine. He would have guessed Hobb—a small, soft, pasty-faced man who always wore a white butcher's apron and a paper hat advertising a local bakery—to be in his sixties, although he and Hobb were exactly the same age. Duncan, who was five years younger, he would have guessed to be far older than himself. Yet it was not vanity but an odd humility and optimism that deluded him: a belief in the wisdom that came with age but had not yet come to him, and a strong faith that one or more new lives awaited him. Indeed, it seemed to him that he had lived a number of lives already, and each new beginning had brought a kind of youth.

When he was ten years old, his father had died, none too well off, and his mother had farmed out her three children to relatives since she was not able to support them herself. So his second new life had begun when he was ten and had arrived by bus in Springdale, a little town fifteen miles from where he presently lived. He'd had a tag around his neck with his name and destination on it, a metal suitcase packed with all his possessions, and a head of hair newly cut, carefully combed, and smelling sweetly of tonic when his uncle came to collect him at the bus depot. His second life had been untroubled, secure, and on occasions, rare and good. It had ended in Korea in the first few minutes of a mortar attack when he'd had part of his head blown away. The first man to him hadn't any doubt he was dead, and the next fellow took the word of the first. They could look right into his skull, after all, so it wasn't surprising. What frail life remained in his body had given no sign, just would not signify. And once they'd tied a tag to his toe, slipped him into a body bag, and set him alongside his tagged and bagged fellows, his reputation for being dead would soon have been fact if he hadn't managed to scare hell out of two men in the quartermaster corps who were heaving bodies into a truck like so many bags of wetwash when he said in a strong, clear voice: "Get your filthy, fucking finger out of my eye!"

The story followed him from aid station to hospital to rehabilitation center like his name, rank, and serial number, but he had no memory of it. In fact his memory was faulty for quite a while after that, and so he had a little trouble isolating just when his third life had started to compose itself. He'd come home with decorations, one eye, and a disability pension. He'd been a terrific pitcher in high school, the best anywhere around, and he'd always thought he'd make his living playing baseball; but, with only one eye, he'd lost his depth perception. He couldn't hit or field very well; and, although his arm was stronger than ever, he'd lost just enough control to make him no better than a thousand other guys. Still, he wasn't the sort to grow bitter. He never could hold a grudge, not about anything. And on the bright side, he had a lifetime disability pension and no longer saw double when he drank too much.

But somehow or other when he was first home and just getting accustomed to being neither in the army nor in a hospital, Louise had snuck up on him. He'd dated her only three or four times in high school and never had anything going with her. How was it that she began to make him feel those few dates were so important? She'd always known he'd come back from the war safe and sound and she'd be able to see him again, she told him. At first he wasn't sure just what to make of such talk and had the constant impulse to look around to see if she weren't talking to some other fellow just behind him. Once or twice he'd gone so far as to suggest that she must have had him mixed up with someone else. But that kind of behavior made her unhappy, and he soon learned not to question the sentiments she claimed to have no matter how unlikely they might seem to him. He found himself feeling guilty, forgetful, insensitive, and hardhearted for not having similar sentiments himself. Somewhere along the line he'd gotten so confused about it all he'd felt obliged to do things to demonstrate the deep regard and affection for her she rightly, and sometimes tearfully, claimed he didn't have. Marrying her was his most desperate effort to prove her wrong. Sometimes he wondered if there was ever another man in the world who had backed himself into such a fix. Louise had claimed he was crazy when he left her; indeed, he feared for a while that she might actually be able to get him committed, since in his heart he suspected she might be right again. But leaving her, for Jesus Christ's sake, wasn't the proof of it. If he was crazy, he'd been crazy for years. What else could you call a fellow who had gotten into the habit of saying and doing just the opposite of what he wanted to say and do? He'd come home from work and find a new rug on the living room floor and Louise already talking before he'd even crossed the threshold. "Oh, I know you'll hate it," she'd say, "and I know we can't afford it." Well, of course he was crazy, since the more he hated it and the more impossible it might be to pay for, the more he'd find himself assuring her it looked real nice and they could manage the payments just fine.

In the years they were married they'd lived in three different houses, each a little larger and more expensive. The first one he'd rather liked. It was a small white frame house, a little tired and sagging maybe, but it had two huge maples towering over it; a big shady porch that ran around three sides; a dilapidated toolshed out back full of rusty nails in jars, spiders, and the damp sweet smell of earth; and a wonderful vegetable garden behind the toolshed. The next one, which she just had to show him but knew he wouldn't like, was a ranch house with aluminum siding, a mimosa tree, and a couple of spindly rosebushes trying to reach the fan-shaped trellises propped on either side of the garage. The third was a large ranch in a new development. It was incredibly hot in the summer and cold in the winter; had four nursery trees, supported by wires and stakes, that never got any higher than his head because they always died and had to be replaced; a cement birdbath in the backyard on which he had not once seen a bird; and a fireplace in the family room that never had anything in it hotter than a dried flower arrangement.

During all that time he'd had a succession of jobs he had no particular talent for, winding up at last as sales manager of the Buick dealership in Springdale, where he spent his days standing around talking nonsense and wearing a snappy sport coat and a prosthetic eye—a troublesome thing that looked any damned place it chose, which Louise had convinced him to endure by pretending he wanted it and was denying himself out of some sort of martyrdom. In fact, the army doctors had been determined to repair his face and give him an eye from the beginning and he wouldn't allow it. He wasn't, himself, exactly sure why; perhaps because the army had already counted him out once, and he didn't want to give anyone a chance to do it again when he might not come around in time to complain.

But he'd give Louise credit. She was a good woman. Decent. Responsible. Not bad looking. Faithful. Hard working. Clean. She'd always had a job, becoming at last an important supervisor with State Farm Mutual. No, he couldn't say she hadn't pulled her share of the load and more. And he couldn't deny they had prospered. They'd sold their first two houses at a considerable profit, and had been offered better than twice what they'd paid for the third. But he couldn't deny either that, over the years, she had been able to disassemble him and put him together again upside down and backward. He claimed to like her hair the way he didn't like it. He'd praise dishes she'd cooked for dinner he hated. He'd spend his vacations and days off with an obtuse and stupefied smile on his face, claiming to enjoy shopping trips, canasta, and other tortures ranging from minor to exquisite.

He began to walk around with the points of his shoulders raised a little toward his ears as though he were frozen in a perpetual shrug. He began to eat antacid tablets so often that the corners of his mouth were forever chalky. Every once in a while he would stammer over the simplest words or the most common, everyday greetings. For no apparent medical reason, pains would often gather around his heart. Even his bowel movements got strange. Sometimes he'd drop pellets like a goat or a rabbit, sometimes a long ropey stool no bigger around than a pencil. Still, every two or three months, seldom more often, he'd get quietly, unconditionally drunk, which would send Louise into a terrible harangue. Yet, ultimately, getting drunk created a little elbow room for him, and although it was only manufactured out of hurt feelings and mistrust and punctuated by sidelong glances, he savored it for the two or three days it would last. He wondered if Louise had been clever enough to suspect the secret, unregenerate life his drunks signified when he himself suspected nothing. Not even the morning he told her he thought he'd just go fishing rather than go to work. It had seemed to him a strange and powerful whim, but nothing more than that. He had turned forty, and it had made him pensive.

Although he'd had no clear idea where he was going, he found himself driving down to Clifton, where his uncle had willed him a piece of land along the river. Not so many years before, his uncle had died a quietly prosperous man and left his children a sizable farm; a large stock barn on the edge of Springdale where animals were auctioned, traded, and sold to market; and some rental property. To Macon, whom he'd raised, he left sixty acres just out of Clifton, fronting the river on one side and the Cove Creek Pike on the other. It was wretched farmland, ledgy and grown up in redbud, dogwood, and oak; and no one thought it was worth a great deal until a Clifton developer realized it was a wonderful setting for expensive houses. One such house had gone up already, another was being built, and he and Louise found themselves in a position to sell three- to five-acre lots for fourteen to twenty thousand dollars each. Lots were being surveyed and roads laid out over the whole parcel, the finest lot reserved, of course, for their fourth house.

When he was in high school, Macon had often gone there to camp and fish. He knew the land well, and it depressed him to see all the fluorescent ribbons tied to trees and the meandering wound bulldozers had made where there would soon be winding roads. There was no pavement beyond the first house, but Macon urged his new Buick over the treach erous road, and when even that played out, over unbroken ground, riding down small bushes and scrub, often scraping the frame, the differential, the oilpan, and God knew what else. Luxuriously the Buick wallowed over terrain it was never meant to travel, but it did not stick, and he was able to drive all the way to the bluff overlooking the river.

He didn't get out of the car for a long while, and when he did, he didn't even think of his fishing gear in the trunk. It took him almost an hour to find and negotiate the nearly impossible route down to the narrow floodplain, but scuffed, skinned, and a bit weak-kneed, he made it. He sat down by the river to catch his breath. But hours later he hadn't moved, and while his glass eye stared off at an idiotic angle, he pondered the unforeseen and ridiculous creature he had become. The afternoon and evening lingered for him as they hadn't done in years. The cicadas sang on and on as he remembered them doing when he was a child, and each change in the quality of light was grave and beautiful. By the time the dew had lifted the smell of grass and earth to his nostrils and the languorous pilgrimage of the river began to shine in the twilight, he knew there was nothing for it but to start all over again.

He spent the first night in the Buick. The next many

nights he spent in a shallow cave two-thirds of the way up the bluff. He made a trip to an Army-Navy store and many trips to a down-at-the-heels hardware store and a lumber company. The Buick suffered tremendous loads of rough lumber tied to its roof and began to bear long scrapes down its flanks from limbs and brush. He bought camping gear, a bucksaw, shovel, ax, block and tackle, logging chain, tarpaper, many boxes of nails and spikes, and other tools and materials, which, grumbling through a hole torn in its muffler and struggling like a fat lady in a mud hole, the Buick conveyed to the edge of the bluff.

Still, he'd been gone eight days before the sheriff and his men showed up just after dark one night. He heard their vehicles coming and had no doubt whom they sought even before he heard them talking over his car.

"Goddamn, it's beat all to hell."

"It's his, though. It's a new one, or it was last week, and them's the right tags."

"I'll be shitfire if I understand it. Where's he at?"

Flashlight beams from the top of the bluff began to probe the floodplain below him and voices began to call his name. He did not answer. He could think of nothing he wanted to say. The little posse spread out along the top of the bluff, shouting and sending shafts of light into the leafy disorder of the dark. Forty-five minutes later they had collected below him to puzzle over tree laps, chips, sawdust, and other evidences of his recent labors; and not long after that, first one flashlight beam and then the others picked out, twenty-five feet above their heads and ten feet above the high-water mark along the bluff, the unfinished underpinnings of the tree house he was building from the mouth of the cave out into the trees growing up from the floodplain. And then the flashlights picked him out, wall-eyed and dirty, squatting in the mouth of his habitation. "Mr. Macon Henslee?" the sheriff had asked. "Speaking," he had answered.

The brand-new life he hadn't quite fit himself into yet, years of saying things he didn't mean, and a little over a week of saying next to nothing had made him peculiar, he realized, or anyway, made him sound peculiar, even to his own ears. But maybe that helped him. Maybe the sheriff and his men just weren't quite sure what he might do, or what he might have up there in his cave to do it with. He refused to be taken home. He refused to admit he was missing, no matter what his wife had reported to the contrary, since he was plainly there for them to see. He refused to come down, or let them come up. He refused to acknowledge that he might need help, or even that he was acting a little strange—he thought it best not to give an inch, since the last time he'd done so, he'd lost nearly twenty years of his life. And finally, somewhat bewildered, angry, and chagrined, the sheriff and his posse left him on his remote perch and went away, their lights and their wry comments bobbing up the bluff a hundred yards to the south where the ascent was easier.

The victory gave him confidence, and for a long time he squatted with his butt resting against his heels, hugging his knees and grinning. There was no law against going fishing, he told himself. No law against how long he might choose to stay. He was on his own land and, by God, sane until proven crazy. He vowed not to give an inch, no matter what. And he vowed not to explain himself, even under torture, since some canny vestigial instinct told him that to do so would open the matter up for discussion and debate. And once that happened, he would become a victim of a logic not his own, and soon thereafter, done for, lost, and a goner once again.

Louise came back the next day with the sheriff, and he had to stick his fingers in his ears and recite aloud to keep her witchery from dragging him down out of the trees and back into his old life. He wished he knew more nursery rhymes, more Bible verses, more anything.

"Hey diddle diddle the cat and the fiddle, the cow jumped over the moon," he told her. "Diddle diddle dumpling, my son John, went to bed with his britches on. Consider the lilies of the field, how they grow. Oh please believe me let me go. Fourscore and seven years ago our fathers brought forth on this continent . . ." and on and on he went until she left.

But of course she came back more nettled and thoroughly outraged than ever. And she sicced all manner of people on him besides, which made it very difficult for him to work on his shelter, since he feared someone might jump out and grab him or throw a net over him. Handcuff him. Stuff him in a straitjacket. And at the approach of anyone, any unidentifiable noise, and sometimes for no reason at all, if he were on the ground, he would drop what he was doing and scramble up into his tree house like a squirrel to sit wild-eyed and atremble, his sides heaving, his heart thumping, and a nervous sweat crawling down his ribs. But he managed to weather visits from all sorts of people who arrived overland and by water: his boss from the Buick place, a marriage counselor, a psychologist from the V.A. hospital, the sheriff, a lawyer, and finally a psychiatrist from the State Board of Mental Health. Even a newspaper reporter from the *Clifton Democrat* as well as the *Nashville Banner* came—two people, anyway, he figured she had not sent to devil him. He had become a local celebrity, and although that annoyed him, he came to realize it protected him too against just the kind of sudden, overpowering attack he most feared. It seemed a shame that his behavior, which he saw as personal, private, and serious, others saw as some sort of joke or stunt, as though he were merely another kind of lunatic flagpole sitter. Still, many of his visitors began to treat him with sympathy, if only because he amused them. Some gave him advice; some brought him good things to eat: pizzas, buckets of fried chicken, baskets of fruit, all of which he desperately needed, since, as frugal as he had been with the initial stores he had bought, he'd also been afraid to risk going to town for any more, and he'd grown grievously thin. The reporter from the *Clifton Democrat* warned him that his wife was out to have him declared mentally incompetent. And even the sheriff, who had started out hugely annoyed, grew considerate—perhaps because he'd gotten his share of publicity—and warned him, man to man, that sooner or later he was bound to find himself in court.

Nevertheless he fought with such weapons as he possessed. He was scrupulously polite to everyone and showed himself willing to discuss any subject calmly and reasonably except his marriage, which he wouldn't discuss at all. Even the psychiatrist from the State Board of Mental Health was not able to declare that he posed any real threat to society, that he was actually dangerous to himself or others.

The psychiatrist—his seersucker suit a little wilted and his glasses a little steamed in the sultry heat of the river bottom—tried diligently to make him admit that his total unwillingness to discuss his troubles with Louise was itself pathological. But Macon insisted it was merely cowardice, since he could no more discuss something with Louise and keep a grip on his own thoughts and desires than he could put a raw oyster in his mouth and decide to swallow only half of it.

Nor did he have to go to court. When Louise determined at last that he was not merely playing some idiotic, protracted joke to annoy her, but that, unthinkable as it was, he meant to live like a hermit, she sent a dry, humorless little lawyer to see him who set about at once telling him he was being sued for divorce and explaining just how much of their common property Louise claimed and fully expected to be awarded. Dirty, impossibly ragged, and no doubt looking maniacal with eyes that peered in two different directions out of his hanging, uncut, uncombed hair, Macon demanded to be set free of all his possessions. He wanted Louise to have the house and everything in it, their savings, their bonds, both cars, and title to all the land his uncle had left him except for the bluff and the six or seven acres of floodplain below it. The little lawyer was shrewd enough to know he'd been conceded far more than he could win in any judgment, a total of something better than a quarter of a million dollars, in fact. He gave Macon one brief, appraising glance, closed his briefcase, and stepped aboard the aluminum motorboat, telling the man he'd hired to bring him upriver to take him back to Clifton.

The next time the little lawyer appeared, a notary public came with him, and in a second boat just behind them was the reporter from the *Clifton Democrat,* the sheriff, and a photographer. There were many papers for Macon to sign, which he hauled up to his tree house in a peck bucket tied to a rope. But when he had signed them all, he let down a ladder he'd made and descended a free man, divested of his property, and, the lawyer assured him, soon to be divested of his wife, since the final divorce would certainly arrive without a hitch. Importantly, gravely, Macon shook hands all around. "Mr. Henslee," the sheriff told him under his breath, "you've let that woman and that little weasel of a Nashville lawyer skin you, son." "Toots," Macon told the sheriff, "I'd like folks to call me Toots."

As for himself, he didn't think he'd ever gotten a better bargain. He had been "Toots" in high school and in the army: an easily contented, optimistic fellow whose life was no more and no less than he chose, at any given moment, to make it; and what price would he consider too much to buy that fellow out of bondage? Why none, he thought, Jesus Christ, none at all. No man there had ever got such a bargain, he suspected, and pitying them, he patted the sheriff's close-shaved, sunburned neck, gave them all a wall-eyed, beatific smile, and explained, if no one minded, that he'd like to take a walk down the Cove Creek Pike and into town.

Two days later he was sitting on the catwalk around his tree house eating peaches out of a can and listening to the cicadas rattle their castanets when a pair of shoes bounced off his roof and pirouetted past the end of his nose. Taking his can of peaches along, he moved to the far end of the catwalk so he could see the top of the bluff, and there was Louise, already heaving off a suit of clothes that folded and furled and landed on the peak of his roof. "You jerk-off, you deceiving son of a bitch!" she shouted, flinging shirts and ties, sportcoats and pants, and finally even a pair of galoshes out into space. "Bum!" she shouted. "Freak!"

True, he thought, all true.

She disappeared, but not for long. "I never want to set eyes on you again," she cried and struggled to the edge of the bluff with something heavy. She swung herself half around heaving his old metal suitcase—the very one he'd had when he was ten—from the brink. The effort caused her to stagger, and for a terrible moment he thought she was going to follow it over the edge, but she didn't. The suitcase hit an outcropping, somersaulted to his roof, slid off the eaves, and fell past him. "You were an ignorant, shiftless nobody when I met you, and this is the thanks I get!"

He had to admit it, she was right again. He struggled for something to say. "Good luck, Louise," he shouted up to her, "and no hard feelings."

"Piss on you! Stay outta my sight!" she shouted back and dashed out the contents of a drawer as though it were dishwater. Rolled socks, handkerchiefs, sunglasses, ball-point pens, rolls of Tums, tie clips, and cuff links bounced and tinkled down the bluff like a miniature avalanche. She disappeared again, and although he ate the rest of his can of peaches waiting for her to return and hoping for a somewhat better good-bye, she didn't come back.

No computer could have retrieved such memories faster than Toots did as he floated beside his johnboat, since, in fact, he didn't have to remember or retrieve them. They were as much with him as his fallen arches, his empty eye socket, the tendency of his smaller toes to rotate to the outside a little more each year. But he took hold of the side of his johnboat and, with a strong scissors kick, heaved both history and flesh over the gunnel. He pulled himself up to the willow by the anchor line and lifted the cinder block into the bow. He wrung out his T-shirt, put the few damp bills and change in its pocket, and hung it over the back of the split-bottomed chair to dry. His hair in a wet, loose ponytail down his back and his beard smelling a little swampy from the river water, he took up his habitual, perfectly familiar position in the chair, picked up his long cedar river paddle, and started the three miles upriver toward home.

By the time he reached the first of his trotlines the effort of paddling and the warmth of the sun had dissolved most of his remaining stiffness, and he was not much worse off for having slept in the bottom of his boat. Still, he was sorry to see the thumb-sized water maple he'd tied one end of his trotline to nodding and jerking. He wasn't in the mood to run his lines just then, but neither did he want to permit needle-nosed gar to rob him, or the caught fish to die. That would attract waterdogs, turtles, and even more gar. Resigned, he moved to the bow of the boat, sculled up to the line, and lifted it into the boat with his paddle. A drum weighing around a pound and a half was hooked on the third dropper from the bank. It wouldn't live to reach his holding pool, and he didn't want it for eating just then, so he unhooked it and let it fin away.

Most of the black sucker minnows had been stripped from his hooks, but a few remained, live and frisky as ever, and toward the middle of the river he lifted aboard a channel cat of about three pounds. After he had pulled the boat from one side of the river to the other by the trotline, he let the line sink again toward the bottom and took up his paddle. Two-thirds of its body out of the bilge water, the channel cat swam from one end of the boat to the other, looking for an exit. From his next trotline he took another small channel cat and a yellow cat of about eight pounds. It seemed only natural, when he would prefer to be napping the day away in his camp, that his lines would hold so many fish. He decided to check his last two lines, transfer his catch to the holding pool, and then spend the remainder of the day at rest and adream. Tomorrow he'd paddle up to Cove Creek, run his minnow traps, and fish properly. The two channel cats and the larger yellow cat struggled about in the bilge and nudged his feet. Under the willows along the shore he heard bluegill and sunfish taking a late, small hatch of may-flies from the surface with delicate sipping sounds. The bright sun dazzled his eye and caused him to sweat, and he scooped a palmful of water from the river and doused his face.

He saw her just after he'd lifted his third line into the boat and started to pull himself across the river. His first thought was that Louise, aggravated by their chance meeting the night before, had come down to the river to bedevil him. But the second glimpse he got as she slipped behind an ancient leaning sycamore told him it wasn't Louise. Louise was duck shaped, and this woman was thin. Anyway, it was nearly half a mile through briars, kudzu, and canebrake from the highway to the river just at that spot, and Louise wasn't about to go to such trouble when she could drive within twenty-five yards of the top of the bluff above his shanty and throw a rock through his roof if it pleased her. Whoever the woman was, she meant to hide from him, that much was certain. What the hell, he thought, hide then; I won't find you.

He took in the trotline with his left hand and paid it out with his right, gliding slowly toward her side of the river where his line was tied to a willow branch close to the sycamore. Toward the middle of the river he lifted a soft-shelled turtle the size of a dinner plate out of the water. It paddled the air frantically with all four feet while he fetched his pocketknife, opened the blade, and cut the dropper. The turtle fell, plop, into the river and disappeared with great speed, the hook still in its throat until such time as it should rust away and the turtle go on about its business. He kept pulling himself along the line toward her hiding place, wondering just what a woman, any woman, could be doing in such a place. The bank was tangled, impossible country to struggle through. He'd never seen anyone along that section, not even to hunt or fish, unless they were in a boat. Could she be lost, he wondered. But then why hide? It made no sense to him. He couldn't see her, but he felt her presence, and by the time he had pulled himself to within a dozen feet of the shore, he could no longer resist speaking. He let his line slip back into the river and sat back on his haunches. "Hydee," he said, "little on the hot side today, isn't it?" The only response from the shore was silence and the heavy odor of greenery cooking in the sun.

He scooped up a palmful of water and doused the back of his neck. As though he'd been asked a question and was obliged to answer, he said, "Well, if you followed the river downstream you'd come to Clifton in about two miles. Upstream is not so good an idea. There's an old iron bridge up that way about four miles and nothing in between except my camp."

The silence behind the sycamore was still as held breath.

"On the other hand," Toots said, "you could put the river at your back and walk straight away from it, and you'd come to the Cove Creek Pike in under half a mile, but it's rough going. Still, if you don't get turned around, that would be the quickest way out."

The current was moving him slowly downstream and he glimpsed the blue hem of a skirt before it retreated clockwise around the sycamore. He stroked his beard. "Well," he said, "if there's nothing further I can do for you, I reckon I'll bid you good day." He knew he shouldn't leave her, but he didn't know what else to do. He didn't want to try to run her down and catch her, and if she didn't want anything to do with him, he supposed he ought to mind his own business and let her mind hers, whatever in the world that might be.

But he'd taken only a single dig with his paddle when she said, "How about across the river, what's over there?"

"Well," he said, "not a great deal. There ain't much but woods up this far. There's a farm a little ways down, and a ways below that you'd come to colored town."

"Oh Christ," she said. "Oh goddamn it anyway."

He held his boat in the current with gentle sculls of his paddle, feeling somehow that he ought to maintain the tree between them if that was her wish.

"You wouldn't have anything to drink, would you? I'm dying of thirst," she said. "Any water or anything?"

"Well, I don't," he said. "I've got a good spring at the camp, though."

"Jesus Christ, Jesus fuckin Christ," she said and began to cry.

While she hid behind the sycamore and cried, Toots held his boat in the current. "Lady," he said at last, vexed and befuddled, "why don't you just come outta there and let me give you a ride down into town."

"I can't," she said and cried some more. Finally he heard her blow her nose. "Oh shit . . . oh . . . ohhhhhh," she said and came into view at last, holding the side of her face and edging down the bank toward the water in what had once been a very pretty blue dress, now thoroughly ruined not only from grass stain, briars, and dirt, but from her own blood. The left side of her face was one round, discolored bruise in which her eye was merely a slit fringed with damp eyelashes, and below that her upper lip was a sad, if ludicrous, balloon. Her nose was bleeding, no doubt from having blown it, and she seemed to brace it tenderly with her fingertips while she crept toward the edge of the river, reaching out at last to take up some water in her hand and wash blood from her upper lip and chin. "Ohhh . . . ohhh . . . ohhh," she repeated as though it were some sort of curative remedy. "Ohhh shit!"

How old was she, Toots wondered, eighteen, twenty, twenty-five? It was hard to tell with her eye swollen shut and her upper lip puffed out like an inner tube. "Young lady," he said, "you get yourself in this boat, and I'll take you to a doctor."

"I fell down," she said, patting river water gently on her face.

"Sure," Toots said, "three or four times, I'd say." He took a dig with his paddle, edged the johnboat into the bank, and carried the split-bottom chair into the bow for her. "Get in," he told her, but she only looked at him, holding her left hand carefully to her nose. "I can't leave you in the puckerbrush," Toots said. "Get yourself in."

"Mister," she said, "do you want to help me?"

"That's what I thought I was doing," Toots said.

"If you want to help me surenuff, you'll let me stay with you till I get cleaned up and have a little chance to think, just a day or two. I won't be any trouble. I'll help your wife do the dishes and all, and you won't even know I'm there."

"I don't have a wife," Toots said.

"I can pay you, not much, but a little," she said and began to weep again, touching the swollen side of her face with her fingertips. "Oh shit, mister, I won't lie. I'm in a peck of trouble, and I've got to hide."

"What kind of trouble?" Toots said.

"Not with the police," she said, "but they can't help me. I've just got to hide. I won't be any bother," she said. "You won't regret it."

But he regretted it already, and while he held the boat against the shore, trying to decide what he should do, his stomach turned a little sour, just as it had in the old days.

"Wait a minute," the girl told him, and taking off her ruined high-heeled shoes, she struggled back up the bank and thrashed around in the bushes a moment before she descended again, dragging a lumpy, flowered laundry bag behind her. Awkwardly she got aboard, put the laundry bag in the chair, and sat on it, paying no mind to the catfish muddling about in the bilge water. "Oh sweet Jesus," she said, "I appreciate this, mister, and I promise you won't regret it."

He considered his fate, gravely wondering if he didn't give off some odor the female of the species could smell, which marked him as an oaf and a fool. It would have to be powerful enough to pull them in from great distances. God knows, down on the river, running his lines and bothering nobody, he hadn't been in this girl's way.

# 3

As for her, sometimes she was horror-stricken and nearly frozen with fear. Sometimes she felt absolutely silly, as though she didn't believe what had happened, as though she thought, somehow, it was all a prank, all somehow perfectly redeemable. She couldn't believe she had stolen his car and hadn't even thought to look at the gas gauge until the engine began to lose power, miss, and finally sputter out; and then to panic and run off in the woods as though they were right behind her when likely no one had the least idea which way she'd gone, Christ Jesus, how dumb. But all the way through Nashville she'd been sure the fancy Lincoln was constantly being recognized—at two in the morning there were few cars on the streets and few people around to see them except just the sort who would recognize Billy Wayne Roland's car and maybe even herself at the wheel. And when the huge yellow automobile had rolled grandly to a stop, her only thought had been to get away from it at once. But what else, she wondered, could she have done? It wasn't as if anyone was likely to give her a ride at that hour, not with her face beaten to a pulp and a laundry bag for luggage.

If only she'd merely left him, but no, she'd had to have one of her insane fits of bravery. Still, by God, nobody was going to treat her the way he'd treated her, not King Kong, not Superman, and least of all Billy Wayne Roland with his fancy suits and silk shirts and gold necklaces and goddamned designer chest hairs. Fuck him.

All at once she came out of her thoughts and realized he was scrutinizing her as if—what with that wild growth of hair and beard—he were an animal peering at her out of a bush. He had set her chair so they were facing each other, and she had no idea what she'd been up to, whether she'd been laughing, crying, or even talking out loud. She thought she ought to speak to him, but she couldn't think of anything to say. "Hi there" didn't seem right, but before she could imagine something better, she saw large, slimy creatures cavorting freely in the bottom of the boat, and she cried out and her feet jumped up. "Christ!" she said, "what are those?"

"Just catfish," he said. "They won't harm you, although you wouldn't want to step on one."

"Don't you worry," she said and hooked her toes over the gunnels on either side of the boat and held her ruined shoes to her crotch to keep her dress down.

Then all at once she felt like crying again. Her nose hurt, her eye ached, her upper lip throbbed with every beat of her heart, and here she was in a leaky boat with a bunch of catfish and a woolly-looking man who might be a freak or a pervert or God knows what, when only the day before she'd been full of hope, safe and sound, and still on the verge of breaking into show business, or so she had thought. She couldn't believe circumstances could change so drastically in only a few hours. She studied the bony, sunburned man kneeling in the dirty water at the end of the boat, suspicious that he might be yet another antagonist, yet another part of life's conspiracy to do her in—a sunken-chested, one-eyed woollybooger paddling her toward some mischief he was trying, at that very moment, to cook up. Well, she wouldn't be taken unaware, she told herself. She'd fight. Sally Ann Shaw was not ready yet, no matter how bad things looked, to kiss her ass good-bye and good riddance. But she began to weep anyway, which made her nose ache as though an icepick were being driven between her eyes toward the very center of her brain.

"Now, now," the woollybooger said to her, "you're already swole up and full of phlegm, crying's only gonna make it worse."

Right, she thought, absolutely right, and she did her best to stop. Tenderly she braced her nose with her fingertips. "So what's your name anyway?" she asked him between catches in her breathing.

"Toots," he told her. "And what's yours?" he said.

She didn't want to tell him her name, and for a moment her stupidity made her feel weak and hollow inside. How could she have provoked such a question? "May," she said at last, stopping just short of giving him the stage name she had invented for herself when she was twelve. How strange that it had come to mind. She had been going to call herself May Morning, but she'd never had the chance to use it, and never even thought of it any longer, although when she'd been a young girl she had invoked that name over and over, adream with visions of herself upon some grand stage, washed in light, flowers in her hair—that was to be her trademark, always to have flowers in her hair—singing of love. Her throat was so dry, it made little cracking noises when she tried to swallow. "How much farther is it to your camp?" she managed to ask.

"Just around the bend," Toots said. "It's not much, I guess, but it suits me well enough. I've never had any company in it."

"If I could get a cold drink of water and maybe lie down for a while, I'd be just fine," she said, since, at the moment, she was feeling very peculiar. Toots, she noticed, had developed a bright halo all the way around him, but so had her toes propped against the gunnels, and a rotten stump sticking out of the water they had just passed. Her forehead felt exceedingly cool although she was sweating. Even the crowns of the trees arranged on either side of the river stood out sharply as though they had been lit from behind, but just as she was noticing that, they began to grow darker. It was so very strange she meant to say something about it, but she didn't get it said.

Toots saw her go pale, but he wasn't prepared for the one eye that wasn't swelled shut to roll white or for her to go suddenly as loose as a rag. First one foot and then the other came unstuck from the gunnels and slapped into the shallow bilge, but at least she remained in the chair. "Well shit," he said.

He could see the pulse jumping in her neck, even from where he squatted, and, paddling carefully so as not to unseat her, he covered the final few hundred yards home. But when he took the last dig with his paddle and ran the bow of the boat up on the muddy little spit of sand in front of his camp, bilge water and catfish rushed forward to swirl around her ankles as the boat slid to a stop, and when the water and fish rushed back toward him again like an ebb tide, she followed, slipping out of her chair as though there were no bones in her body so that she flopped helter-skelter on the wet, dirty floorboards drained by the tilt of the boat. "Shitfire," he said and stepped over the gunnel into the shallow water.

He got in the bow behind her and set the chair out on the sand bar, but he hadn't noticed that her head was resting on the bottom rung, and when he moved the chair with her laundry bag on it, her head thumped against the floorboards like a bowling ball. "Mercy," he said. He wiped his hands up and down his thighs as though to clean them and tried to figure out just how best to take hold of her.

She was so supple and limp she was difficult to manage, but finally he got her sitting up, locked his arms beneath her breasts, and backed out of the boat. Her heels made little trails across the sand and fainter marks up the bank all the way to the tree house. Gently he deposited her there while he held his chin and took thought. Years ago he'd rigged a trap door and a block and tackle to raise a wood cookstove into his house and had retained it to lift great loads of firewood, but she was altogether so loose and soft and supple he didn't quite want to trust her to a rope sling for fear the hemp ropes would damage her skin, or else she'd slither out and fall. He sucked his teeth and studied her. "Well, shoot," he said. He went around in front of her, propped her knees up, stood on her toes, took her wrists, heaved her upright, and squatted so that she collapsed over his shoulder. With her head hanging down his back and his arm between her legs so that he could hold her right hand with his, he made a kind of haversack out of her and climbed the ladder. She smelled of sweat and super-heated perfume, and he grew a little dizzy with it. She wasn't very heavy, but he only had one hand free for the ladder, and it was arduous labor to get her in the tree house, but finally, as though he were putting to bed an enormous baby he had burped, he was able to deposit her, almost gently, on his bunk. She was still breathing and her color seemed a little better, but she showed no sign of coming around. "Mercy," he said in a winded voice, fetched a peck bucket, and went out along the catwalk to his spring.

Nervously he bounced his shoulders up and down, trying to settle them more comfortably, but the notion that some feminine witchery might be seeking a grip on him seemed to dicker with his backbone. He held the bucket under the pipe from his spring, and when it was half full, set it aside and drank from his cupped hands and splashed his face as though to wake himself from a dream. But when he got back inside and set the bucket beside the bunk, she was just as he had left her. He found a glass, a tin of aspirin, and a clean dish towel. He dipped her a drink of water, put it aside on a rough little table he'd made, and sat down beside her, wondering just what sort of nonsense she'd been into to get herself so abused. Her wishes to the contrary, he thought he'd better fetch her a doctor somehow. Likely she had a concussion or she wouldn't just pass out; although it was possible, he supposed, that struggling through the thick tangle along the river with the sun beating down the way it had been, she'd had some sort of heatstroke. Any fool could see she wasn't in the best condition for a hike. But hell, for all he knew, having a heatstroke might be worse yet. He tore his dish towel into sections and, dipping one in the cold spring water, he began, with clumsy gentleness, to wash her face. She did not come around. He didn't know what else to do. He didn't think it was a good idea to leave her, but he suspected he ought to climb the bluff, hurry to the nearest house, and call the hospital.

He thought he remembered from his army first aid training that propping the feet up was a good idea—it got more blood to the head or something of the sort—so he fetched the cushion out of his one comfortable chair and his winter jacket from a nail along the wall where his few clothes were hung. Awkwardly, apologetically, he moved her legs to one side, positioned the cushion and his rolled-up jacket, and rested her dirty feet on the prop. It seemed to him he remembered that cooling the wrists was a good way to cool the blood, and he wet two more rags and wrapped them around her wrists, but then he was sure he remembered that unconscious people ought to be kept warm. Well hell, he thought, should he cover her with something? It was crazy to put cold rags on her to cool her and then cover her up to keep her warm. But just at that moment she jerked awake.

"Hey," he said and smiled, "I was nearly . . ." but she flew at him, batting the air in front of his nose with one wild swing and swatting his beard with another.

"Back off, you son of a bitch!" she shouted.

He stumbled away with his palms raised. "Whoa," he said. "Jesus, girl, you take one kind of a fit after another." He retreated to a chair beside his kitchen table and sat down while she glared at him as though she just might leap into pursuit and claw him to ribbons. "There's you some water," he said, flipping his index finger toward the glass, trying to calm her by being calm, "and I found some aspirin if you want them."

The fierceness left her face so suddenly it seemed to take the color with it, and he thought she was going to faint again, but she merely gazed about the room and back at him. "God," she said, "I'm sorry. I'm really, really sorry. I couldn't think who you were for a second." She found the glass of water and drank half of it, found the tin of aspirin, put a tablet on her tongue and washed it down. "I didn't mean to fight at you, honest," she said. When she had taken two more aspirin, she said, "I guess I passed out, huh?"

"You went pale as clabbered milk and keeled over," he said and tilted his head to one side thoughtfully. "I don't like that, missy. I'm not much at doctoring. I was getting ready to hunt a telephone and call the hospital."

"Please," she said. "I won't pass out anymore, I promise. I won't act crazy. I'll lie right here on this bunk and rest. Please."

When she talked her upper lip stuck out at an even more ludicrous angle, seemed, indeed, to wave in the breeze like the lip of a nickering horse. Somehow it was very difficult to refuse a person who looked so altogether foolish. "Shoot," he said.

"Thank you," she said. "I'll pay you. I'll see that you don't lose by it."

He shook his head. "Money's not . . ."

"Where's my bag?" she said suddenly, propping herself up in bed.

"Down at the boat," he said. "I haven't had time . . ."

"I better get it," she said and swung her legs off the cot.

"Jesus Christ, I'll get it," he said. "You fall out again, and I won't guarantee you won't wake up in the county hospital."

"All right," she said. "I'll stay right here. I won't move a muscle."

Toots climbed down the ladder and descended the path past the holding pool, feeling a little shaky himself, as though, given just the right provocation, he might turn his own toes up and faint dead away. Somehow the girl had spooked him, and spooked him still, though at least, on the slim evidence of the fire in her, he felt a little better about her health. It was just that he had lived so long in his hermitage, her presence unnerved him.

As though they were content to wait for a rain that would raise them up and out of the boat, the catfish were resting quietly in the bilge until Toots loomed over them. Then they made a ruckus, one of the smaller ones charging ahead to skid out of the water and across the damp floorboards to the very bow of the boat. Careful not to get finned, but with expert ease, he caught them and pitched them into the holding pool, although no doubt they would have lived through the night rebreathing the same exhausted water over and over again.

The sun, still high, had nevertheless dropped behind the bluff so that shadows spread across the tree house and floodplain, as well as his muddy little spit of sand where three wooden boats and one aluminum semi-V hull were beached and tethered—all four boats having washed down to him in the flood waters of one spring or another from far upriver where they had broken free. He had captured over a dozen boats through the years. Some he had relinquished to their owners who claimed them; some he had sold; some, unclaimed and unwanted, like these, remained. He considered them a moment, although to what purpose, he didn't know and couldn't say, and he considered the aspect of his habitation: the fine spring he had made by hammering a long star drill into a narrow, mossy fissure until it would accept a pipe—long since mossy-throated too—where before the water had merely fanned out to keep a wide section of the bluff dripping and slimy; the springhouse he had built at the base of the bluff to keep his perishables cool, which was fed by a trough from the pipe and made of mortar and stone to survive the floods that often covered it; his holding pool where his fish were kept alive for the market, which was fed by the runoff from the spring house and which, every March without fail, was silted in by floods; the tree house itself, sparsely furnished with a few chairs and a table he'd bought from a secondhand furniture store, his wood stove, and other items of his own manufacture, but nevertheless comfortable; the small cave from which the tree house extended—furnished with a bunk too, and shelves made from driftwood the river brought him every spring, and a fire pit below a natural if deviously crooked chimney that leaked smoke from half a dozen places along the top of the bluff. Far above him the crowns of the tallest trees glowed in the sun. Around him cicadas whirred and whirred again while winsome solitude—the finest of all women—withdrew upriver to make room for the mistreated girl. Scratching his beard thoughtfully, plucking the end of his nose, he stared upriver after her as though he had only just missed her. For certain he could still smell her fragrance on the air. But then he came to himself and, feeling altogether foolish, he shouldered the lumpish, flowered laundry bag and set the split-bottomed chair back in the johnboat. Nervousness dickering with the set of his shoulders, he went back up the path trying to figure out how he should behave, wondering if he should offer to fetch some water and heat it so the girl could take a bath, wondering what he could fix for supper that wouldn't be difficult for her to eat.

As for her, she was still trying to clear her head of visions of Billy Wayne Roland, of the absolute monster he had turned out to be. She had awakened with Toots bending over her, reliving the beating Billy Wayne had given her. He had called her a proud little slut, and in her present mood, she supposed, if there could be such a thing—and she knew there certainly could—then that was what she was. "Agent, my ass," she'd shouted into his face, "you're not a goddamned thing but a pimp and a pusher." But she'd known that for a long time, or at least she'd known he was a pimp and a pusher; she'd merely thought that being a pimp and a pusher was maybe an ordinary sideline to being an agent in the country music business. "I sell satisfaction, you dumb cunt," he'd told her and slapped her into the birdcage so that she and Freddy fell together, only somehow one of the parakeet's wings had gotten through the bars and the whole weight of the cage was lying on it so that he fluttered pitifully, flipping about as though he'd surely wrench the wing out by its fragile moorings. She'd been trying to lift the cage so the bird could free itself when he'd dragged her up from the floor by the hair of her head. "Cocksucker" she called him and tried to knee him, but his fist drove pain, bright as neon and red as blood, through her eye and deep into her head. He cursed her and tore her clothes and hit her until she realized, although she was no more than half-conscious, he'd got beyond mere anger and was making some kind of hideous love to her, that his blood was up and he was aroused. Although what he uttered to her was as vicious and vile as he could make it, there was the urgency and tone of love in it. Although he gave her as much pain as he could, he was giving most of it in latitudes meant for caresses. Of course, the son of a bitch! She'd suspected before that Billy Wayne Roland couldn't quite tell the difference between brutality and lovemaking, but she hadn't let herself admit it. After all, at moments all through her life she'd felt the hint of it in other men. Somehow, all at once, that realization had snapped her fully conscious and torn such a cry from her throat that no animal fighting for its life could have outdone the sound of it. But when he struck her next, she felt teeth break loose from their sockets and something crack in her nose. He flung her on the daybed and ripped at her skirt and underclothes. And then he was behind her and had the hair of her head twisted in his fist and her head wrenched back, and there was the sudden outrageous pain and humiliation of his entering where she had never been entered before.

Lying on her bunk in Toots' shack, she decided he should have killed her. She wondered what he could have been thinking to stay in her apartment and drink himself into a snoring, contented sleep, like some husband who'd come home from a hard day's work, had a little sex and a few beers and gone to sleep in front of the television, content to fart, snort, and snore until the little woman should wake him up to go to bed. Did he think nothing of any real importance had happened? Did he think he'd put her in her place and would have no more trouble out of her? Did he think she'd liked it?

When she awakened and discovered she was alive, that

Billy Wayne hadn't broken her neck, or her back, or even, at last, her spirit, when she discovered she could move, however painfully, she knew she was going to take a terrible revenge. The strange bravery she'd owned ever since she was a child puffed itself up, filled her breast like helium, and made her giddy. Quietly, she'd gone into the bathroom and cleaned herself as best she could. She'd put on her finest dress, knowing she was going to take the attaché case he'd set aside when he'd first come in, already half-drunk and bragging that he was going to buy enough coke with what was in it to keep every producer, promoter, singer, song writer, and back-up-fucking-guitar-player in Nashville two feet off the floor for months. And she knew she was going to take his car. She supposed she'd known she was going to knock hell out of him as a final parting gesture. Anyway she'd known it when she'd come back into the room and seen Freddy Fender—who had always been so sleek and pert—disarrayed, damp from his spilled water dispenser, and already stiffening into a corner of his littered cage.

Billy Wayne was sprawled asleep in a chair, his trousers in a discarded heap where he had kicked them off—no doubt just pleased as hell with himself—rather than pull them up. The scene told all: beating her up, raping her, buggering her had been very satisfying but exhausting work, after which, Billy Wayne needed a little rest and couldn't be bothered to put his pants on. Even his cock lay where it had wilted back toward the fly of his electric blue hip-hugging jockey shorts, pale and soft and innocent as you please.

He roused while she was going through his pants for the car keys, grinned at her, not quite realizing what she was up to. "Hey baby . . ." he'd said and said no more, since she'd already dropped his trousers, plucked the heavy brass lamp off the table beside him, and started a swing that would bash him into the middle of next week. She was ready and willing to hit him again, but he didn't seem to need it. Yet hitting him rushed her departure, scared her. Although she still felt giddy and brave, she wasn't about to pull down the little trapdoor in the hallway ceiling and climb up for her suitcase, for sure. She threw half a dozen things in a laundry bag, taking her lamp with her everywhere she went in case he should need another bash with it. She kept an eye on him, mad as hell, scared, and shaking from her odd combination of giddiness and bravery. Finally she sacked up his attaché case, and then, standing over him, suddenly full of pain and outrage all over again, she thought: there, you bastard! Nobody beats and buggers Sally Ann Shaw and gets away with it! Not nobody!

He lay sprawled in the chair, much as before, even a little rattle in his breathing that was almost, if not quite, equivalent to a snore—a little rattle that was most likely the tail end of the remark he had been about to make to her when she'd hit him with the lamp, and so, converted whatever the condescending, wise-assed remark might have been to a little bubble of spit, lodged in his throat and aggravated by the breath left in him. She looked down on him, his electric blue silk shirt unbuttoned below his breastbone, the gold chain nestled in his perfectly masculine chest hair, his electric blue hip-hugging shorts with the limp, innocent penis peeking out, and she remembered him wrenching her head back by her hair, until she would have passed out from that alone if it weren't for the pain his thrusts sent through her as though she were being impaled with lightning—pain through which she could feel, nevertheless, his pleasure—and she knew that what she had done to him was not nearly enough. Killing him wouldn't even have been enough.

The sudden, virulent inspiration had gone through her like electricity. She dropped her laundry bag but took the lamp with her into the bathroom and returned with a thermometer, which she inserted as though it were a practiced art. When she crushed the thermometer inside his penis, he merely shuddered and paled and his lips turned dark blue. She had expected him to roar up out of unconsciousness like a bull, and she had snatched up her lamp in order to do battle. But there was no need, and she left him, suddenly so shaky with the passing of her inspired anger and bravery that she could hardly negotiate the stairs down to the street.

She couldn't believe, even now, that any of it had happened. But she knew it had. It had happened because her body still bore the pain, because she was hidden away with this strange fellow who called himself Toots and who, even now, was coming through the door with her flowered laundry sack over his shoulder.

# 4

She was relieved when she discovered that two teeth she thought she might lose were tightening up again. She peered into a hand mirror Toots kept on a shelf over the washbasin and pushed gently on the teeth with her forefinger, but they moved only a little. And her eye had opened enough so that a slit of it showed: a bedazzled iris and pupil and a sliver of red as bright as a ruby where the white should have been. But she could see out of it. When she closed the good one and looked about, she could see a bit of the world, although it was stalked top and bottom with blurred eyelashes big as tree limbs. Still, her upper lip remained puffed and largely wrong side out so that she looked ludicrous and simple-minded, although it didn't actually hurt much. Mostly it felt heavy. The colors of her face, however, were fantastic, a starburst running from purple through red and yellow to green. She had no notion how long it would take before she could walk down a street without attracting startled second glances from everyone she met. When her eye opened up a bit more and her lip went down, it was possible she could disguise the rest with makeup and sunglasses. Maybe, she thought, while she studied herself in the small, cheap hand mirror, she ought to dye her hair brown since that was the color it wanted to be. She'd been lightening it so long she wasn't even quite sure how dark it would become if she allowed it its way—the dull mousy color of her pubic hair maybe.

She peered at herself in the mirror, feeling as if she were making some sort of hideous face, except the ugly, mis-shapen visage looking back at her stubbornly refused to unmake itself. She put the mirror away in disgust and went out upon the catwalk, where two pots of bathwater had been set on a camp stove to heat. Toots had dragged out a galvanized washtub, fetched her some water, and gone off to run minnow traps and set trotlines up the river. "I'll not show up again for two or three hours," he'd told her, rubbing the back of his neck and looking away in his shy, awkward, decorous fashion. She stuck her finger in one of the pots and found it still only lukewarm, and since the washtub waiting in the middle of the room was nearly half full of spring water, she figured she'd better let the pots come to a boil if she wanted a hot bath.

Anyway, she wanted to try once again to open Billy Wayne Roland's briefcase. During the past two days when Toots had gone to sell his fish and pick up groceries, or run his lines, or merely gone off as though on purpose to allow each of them to be alone, she'd had any number of opportunities to get into it. But she'd let most of them go by out of some queer dread. She felt peculiarly unwilling to confront what she had stolen from him as though out of revulsion for the act that had provoked her to take it, as though as long as the briefcase remained unviolated, she might somehow magically be able to undo the whole string of events. But she knew she was being silly and childish, and on a sudden impulse she went into the single large room of the tree house and dragged the laundry bag from under her cot and withdrew the briefcase. It was made of a very tough brown plastic material that was textured like leather and virtually indestructible. In two or three halfhearted attempts to open it, she had only scratched the metal around the two combination locks trying to jimmy the thing open with a screwdriver. She had found the screwdriver in a toolbox in the cave where, each night, Toots crept away to sleep, and she went into the cave and got the toolbox again and sat down to ponder its contents. There was a file, but she couldn't figure out how to attack the briefcase with it; and there were a hammer, three or four screwdrivers, pliers, and a hacksaw among other tools she didn't recognize.

She decided to try the hacksaw, but she couldn't work it very well since the briefcase kept moving about or falling over before she could make a single smooth stroke. Finally she sat on her cot, held the case between her feet, and set the saw blade against the metal closure, hoping ultimately to saw through the fingers of the lock; but after only a few strokes, the thin blade of the saw bound and broke. "Fuck it," she said and threw the saw down in disgust. After a moment of petulance during which her eyes welled up and the bad one leaked sticky tears upon her swollen cheek, she snatched up the hacksaw and broken pieces of blade, put them back in the toolbox, and picked out the largest screwdriver and a hammer. She tried to hammer the edge of the screwdriver into the closure by one of the combination locks, and ultimately she succeeded, but no matter how she twisted and pried, the lock would not give way, and she only managed to make a small, twisted hole between the metal lips of the closure. She yanked the screwdriver out and struck the combination lock an angry blow with the hammer, but that merely caused the briefcase to bounce up from the floor as though it were made of rubber. She hit it again, and it bounced and fell on its side, and she beat the side of it ineffectually until at last she flung the hammer across the room. She glared at the briefcase as though it were Billy Wayne himself, despising it, determined now to open it no matter what.

Goddamn it, she needed things. She had taken only her two best dresses and her laciest underwear, so that she went about Toots' shack like a fancy doll some child had dressed for a party. She needed some jeans and T-shirts, some shorts, some underthings, some sneakers, some shampoo, makeup, a goddamned toothbrush. She stared at the briefcase and wept. "You son of a bitch!" she said and looked wildly about the room for something she could use to do violence to it. In a box by the wood stove she spied a hand ax and fetched it at once. She set the briefcase on edge and took careful aim at the combination lock closest to her. Her butt in the air and both hands gripping the handle of the ax, she gave it a chop. Resilient as the case was, it didn't spring back to its original shape after that, although it didn't open either. She chased it about the room, setting it up and chopping at it as though it were something alive she meant to kill. Sometimes she missed altogether and chopped the floor; sometimes she chopped it as it lay flat before she bothered to set it upright again. Bending over in such a fashion made her eye hurt, and so did the vibrations of her blows, and she wept copiously and cursed as she chased the briefcase about and pounded at it as though she were trying to kill a mouse with a broom. When it came open at last, she didn't notice right away and gave it two or three extra blows just as she might have given a dead mouse two or three extra blows. "My God," she said, weeping and sniffing and wiping at tears and the liquor from her nose tinged pink with blood. Bundles of twenty-dollar bills with bands around them were scattered about the gashed, wrecked case, yet there seemed to be no room inside it to hold any more money than it still contained. She had never seen so much money, never even imagined so much. "Oh Christ," she said and sat down cross-legged with the ax in her lap, "oh shit." She wiped her nose on the back of her wrist. She didn't know what she had expected, ten thousand dollars maybe, maybe even twenty-five. The trouble with an asshole like Billy Wayne was that you never knew when to take him seriously. She would have been less surprised if the briefcase had been empty—but this, this was altogether unimaginable. She felt as if she had robbed Fort Knox.

She picked up the bundle closest to her, counted it, and found it contained a thousand dollars. She counted bundles of twenties by two until she reached one hundred thousand and then guessed at what remained: another hundred thousand easy, maybe more. For a long moment she sat perfectly still. Her good eye stared blankly at nothing. The bad one, puffed and puddled, was all but sightless again. Whatever notions she'd had that he might not come after her—that waking up with a cock full of broken glass and alcohol, his traveling bordello of a car and his briefcase gone, might teach him a lesson, might teach him, by God, that Sally Ann Shaw was not someone he could mess with—all those notions left her at once. He'd come after her, all right, and he'd kill her when he found her. "Oh boy," she muttered. But then she scrambled up, emptied the briefcase into her laundry bag, gathered Toots' ax and tools, and put everything back in its proper place. Feverishly, nearly falling, she climbed down out of the tree house with the wrecked briefcase, intending to drop it to the bottom of Toots' outhouse, but it wouldn't go through the hole. It had seemed the perfect place. No one would ever look for anything down there. But she could find no quick way to get the briefcase into the ghastly, stinking pit, so she took it a short distance down the floodplain and covered it with dirt and leaves, only to uncover it again when she saw how perfectly obvious it was that something was buried there. Finally, on the riverbank she gathered stones, got one of the combination locks to take hold again, and heaved the weighted briefcase into the water. Perversely it floated for a few seconds before, giving up a sigh of bubbles, it tipped, hung a moment more just below the surface, and sank.

Her heart pounding, she hurried back to the tree house and scrambled up the ladder. She snatched up her laundry bag and looked about the room. Her muddy shoes were on the floor by the foot of the bed, and she scooped them up and put them in the bag, thinking it best to stay barefooted until she reached pavement somewhere. The dress she'd worn that first day was hanging on a nail, and she snatched it down, but it was so stained and picked, she decided—with a tug of sorrow all out of proportion to its value as well as her present circumstances—to poke it through the hole in Toots' outhouse. Trembling, her heart fluttering like a bird in a cage, she looked about the room again to make sure she was leaving nothing behind. But no, it wouldn't be right to merely disappear, she decided. For Toots' sake as well as her own she knew she ought to leave him a message. She found a stub of a pencil in an empty coffee can on the windowsill, found a paper bag, and sat down to scribble him a note. *Dear Mr. Toots,* she wrote, *I'm in bigger trouble than I told you, and I can't stay here anymore. Bad people might come looking for me, but you should not tell them anything or that you ever even saw me at all. I broke your saw and chopped your floor, but I will leave some money for your trouble and for taking me in which was a gentlemanly thing to do. Wait a long time, even a year, before you spend it, never tell anyone that you ever saw me, and thank you for being real nice.* She signed it *May Morning.* She took a bundle of twenties from her laundry bag, thought a moment, and took another. "What the hell," she said and plopped them down firmly on her note. Grabbing up her laundry bag, she rushed out on the catwalk to the ladder before she stopped in her tracks. Jesus, she thought, Jesus Christ, she was doing it again. When the car had first run out of gas, she could have walked into town and waited at the bus station for hours with very little danger, no matter that she looked a sight. But now, after Billy Wayne's car had been on the side of the road almost three full days, it was certain to have been discovered. And if it had been dumb to run off in the woods when the car had stopped, and she knew it had, then it was suicidal and insane to walk out in plain sight three days later. She might as well have written Billy Wayne a letter and told him she'd wait until he caught up before she started to run again. She carried the laundry bag and her blue dress back inside again, dumped them on her bunk, and sank down beside them. "Christ Jesus," she told herself, "I've got no sense at all, no more than a pissant, no more than a graham cracker." She began to tremble and shake and make a strange noise she couldn't recognize as either purely laughter or weeping. There was nothing to do, she thought, but wait it out. There was nothing to do but hope that Billy Wayne and the hoodlums who worked for him wouldn't figure her to be within five hundred miles of that yellow Lincoln. And she wouldn't have been if she'd had her wits about her. How could anyone believe she'd steal a fortune, drive scarcely forty miles in Billy Wayne's circus of an automobile, park it in plain sight of everyone, walk off a little ways, and settle down like a bird on a nest. Goddamn! Suffering Jesus nailed hand and foot! Who would believe such a thing? She made the noise again that was neither quite laughter nor weeping. Naw, they'd be expecting her to turn up in Atlanta, Memphis, Miami Beach maybe, but certainly they wouldn't expect her to be where she was. All she had to do was stay absolutely out of sight and figure out just how to handle Toots. Figure out what to tell him so he'd let her stay on and not give her away through some sort of carelessness. Feeling very shaky, as though she were having a chill from the inside out, she rose from the bunk and collected her note and the bundles of twenties and stowed them away in her laundry bag again, and stowed the laundry bag under her bunk. She heard a slight noise and thought for a moment that it might be some new noise she herself was making, but it was only the two pots of water Toots had put on for her bath, boiling now, the pots themselves chattering a little against the grill of the stove.

# 5

Two minnow buckets in his left hand and a seine over his right shoulder, Toots waded upstream. The creek ascended from its confluence with the river in a series of pools and shallow, ledgy riffles, but the few small schools of minnows he saw were not worth the trouble. They scattered ahead of him like star bursts, having lost the faith that kept them all together when their numbers were larger. Crawdads darted backward along the bottom. Now and again a snake would plop into the water from a low overhanging limb where it had been sunning, or another, already in the stream, might poke its head above the surface to take Toots in before it ducked and wrinkled away. He saw all those things, but in some deeper station of his brain he was pondering the girl, who, for two days now, had occupied his camp. Sleek as a deer she was, out of place as some rare tropical bird, and distrubing as a gnat trapped and mucking about in the inner chamber of his ear. She troubled his sleep. She made him feel awkward in his own habitation, responsible for gestures he would have had to guess at ten years ago when he'd lived a life that required them, just the life he'd given up and didn't miss. Indeed, when he considered his years with Louise and even the years before he was married, he felt smug. These days if he wanted to go on a toot, he went on a toot; and when it was over, he could lie around all day and moan if it pleased him, and often it did. To be nailed to his cot with his mouth parched, his stomach queasy, and the relentless pain of a hangover gripping his head, seemed, now and again, just what was wanted. It was a religious experience, by God, to lie there and decide if life was worth the living without being harangued by a woman or otherwise having the issue clouded by obligations of business, bills, ambitions, or irrelevant responsibilities. Under those conditions, he had always been able to make the tentative affirmation that it was—at least until the next toot when the question might reassert itself. Hell, it was a pleasure to be born again in such a fashion and—feeling frail and new and outfitted with senses that were rubbed raw and tender—wash the stink of one's debauchery away, maybe have a cool glass of buttermilk and a piece of cornbread and watch the tarnished light of day descend from behind the bluff across his hermitage and the river. Who could want a better life? He wasn't sure there was one. His pain and his pleasure were of a very simple order—were often one and the same, or at least so dependent on one another that to lose one would be to lose the other as well. How else to understand the cold serenity of a hoarfrost on a December morning without having his breath smoke, his body shiver inside the blanket lining of his jumper, his wet fingers ache at running his lines? How else to explain the anathema of a bottle of whiskey? Or the pleasure of warmth when there wasn't first cold, or eating when there wasn't first hunger. Or going off to a Nashville whorehouse, for that matter, without the benign misogyny of his solitude.

Nine years had given him plenty of time to speculate, to grow peculiar, to pare his prejudices and pleasures down to fighting trim. He'd all but weaned himself from frills and niceties, since it was his notion they brought more trouble than satisfaction. He'd gotten as cagey as a feral cat. He could easily have afforded a car, but if he had a car, he'd have to support and maintain it, buy insurance and deal with other worrisome matters; and who was to say he wouldn't soon decide he needed a better one—more comfortable, faster, quieter, prettier—no sir, by God, he'd ride the bus. More than once he'd thought of buying a small outboard engine to ferry himself up and down the river, but they were noisy, smelly machines that needed gas and oil and broke down, and, in any case, offered him only speed, which, for a man in his position, was a useless commodity. He needed to have something to eat. He needed a place to keep himself from the weather. Beyond that, he needed very little—something to turn his hand to, peace, time to speculate. The simple fact was, he was easily contented; and, left to his own devices, never bored. There was, he suspected, something subversive in all of this, something that threatened the fabric of commerce, perhaps the whole fabric of civilization, which was, he suspected, a house of cards in any case, built on silly urges for acquisition that could never quite satisfy and false ambitions that, whether achieved or not, turned hollow. How else to explain the inevitable collapse of so many grand societies?

"Ha," he said aloud and waded on up Cove Creek, gesturing with his minnow buckets to an elderberry thicket. Somehow, he supposed himself to be still pondering the girl—at that moment no doubt bathing in the water he had fetched and put on to heat for her—as though he had beautifully analyzed the nature of her threat to him and, incidentally, discovered the basic flaw in the body politic. But his thinking was often as devious and oblique, since, for a long time, there had been no one to point out to him how he had strayed from his subject. Indeed, often in pondering the smallest anomaly—why someone might cry when they were happy, or laugh when they were sad—he might come to a totally new understanding of, say, the State of Israel, an understanding so brilliant as to set him up for an afternoon, although the trail of his proofs would have disappeared by the time he reached his conclusion, and the conclusion itself, if he could even remember it the following day, would seem either bland or obtuse.

Trouble was, women were not so easily contented. He suspected they were the secret props of every society. He suspected, as well, that they were generally more intelligent than men, less forgiving, more devious; and capable, at last, of the ultimate trick: the ability to turn weakness into strength, so that any fellow who did not wish to harm them or make them unhappy would find himself taken prisoner, wrapped like a fly in a web, all google-eyed and bumfuzzled and unable even to wipe the paralytic smile from his face. Piss on that. He didn't want one in his tree with him.

Still, they were the stuff of his dreams, and he admired every line of them. They pleased the eye. They smelled good, tasted good, were pleasant to the touch, and carried with them warm, sweet sockets of pleasure. But he didn't want one of his own. He wanted to rent.

As a consequence, every few months he'd scrub himself down with bath soap, rather than the Octagon he favored. Shave. Tie his hair back in a ponytail. Put on dress pants and a dress shirt, leather shoes, and a velvet eye patch (all of these niceties remaining from the time Louise had showered them upon his roof from the top of the bluff). And catch the bus to Nashville, where, on a back street, he'd ring the bell of what had once been a fine Georgian mansion, now an equally fine whorehouse. Because he was polite, gentle, and extremely easy to please, he'd become a favorite customer, as well as a standing joke. "Sugar," he'd heard one of the girls tell another he'd chosen for the night, "about all you have to do to get him off the first time is shake his hand and say, 'Hi.' Lord God, but he's a horny old thing."

Where the hell were the black sucker minnows, he wondered. He sat down on a rock and took off his basketball shoes in order to wash out the fine sand that mysteriously got inside to crowd his toes. Deerflies circled his head in lazy orbits, and somewhere away a meadowlark made music. Oddly he was annoyed almost as much by one as by the other. Somehow they made him feel he ought to be somewhere else; somehow they made him feel lonely. But as soon as he registered the thought, he dismissed it. Deerflies, meadowlarks, the endless ascending riffles and pools of Cove Creek stretching before him, the sunlight glittering indiscriminately in the trees, none of those things had the power to make him feel lonely. They were merely the quiet stage, the neutral background for whatever set of feelings might comfort or afflict him. It was the girl. He refused to consider the matter further, laced up his shoes, and went on up the creek, the notion haunting him that a man might only choose to be one sort of fool or another. And if one considered the problem too deeply, even the matter of choice might seem to be in doubt.

But she would leave soon. It was ridiculous to think otherwise. And when she was gone, he could settle down again to the quiet rhythm of his solitary days. He tried to be pleased with the thought and tried not to consider that, when she left, whatever he did, he would do in the absence of her and that it would not quite fill up time and be adequate to its own purpose. Perhaps, he thought, he should go to another place, to Louisiana, say, and find himself a swamp and learn to live there, construct himself a house of reeds and thatch perched on stilts above the still water, live on crayfish and frogs, watch the wide sunset mark the flight of cranes and transfix Spanish moss, bald cypress, and loblolly pine; or maybe he should go to Alaska and make himself a house of snow or skins, learn to outwit wolves and arctic fox, eat willow leaves, waylay the caribou and salmon, watch the moon sail endlessly above the blue-white geography of snow, learn to live with perfect solitude until, at last, she locked his lifeless bones in ice.

He went on up Cove Creek arguing with himself, muttering aloud and gesturing with his minnow buckets and seine, weaving fantasies, snorting with humor, blushing; so that anyone who might have chanced to see him would have had no doubt he was a madman.

At last, a mile and a quarter from the river, he came across a school of black sucker minnows so vast they moved as one organism. They furled and folded and swarmed upstream, now and again flashing, all together, a glint of their silver sides. He shook out the stale, wet weave of his net and seined his buckets full.

# 6

"How come Mr. Billy Wayne Roland didn't come down to pick up his own car?" the deputy said.

"He's sick," Jerry said.

Esco gave a soft snort of laughter from where he leaned against the doorjamb of the stuffy little office, and the deputy looked at him a moment, trying to judge his intent or catch the joke.

"I've got the title with me," Jerry said and plucked the title from the pocket of his beige linen jacket and pitched it on the counter before the deputy.

"There didn't seem to be no registration in the car," the deputy said. He was copying down information from the title onto a note pad with a pencil. "That's not legal," he said without looking up.

"There's a vanity mirror on the passenger's sun visor," Jerry said; "the registration's behind the mirror."

The deputy cocked an eyebrow, and, without looking at either of them, strolled across the office and sat down at a desk by a window that looked out on the courthouse square. He was suspicious, Jerry could tell, and Jerry blamed Esco, who looked exactly like what he was, a cheap thug and a dealer. Esco leaned against the doorjamb in his powder blue leisure suit and purple shirt with powder blue diamonds on it, no doubt bought as a matching set on sale, a sixty-nine ninety-five value marked down to twenty-nine ninety-five. Of course the circumstances of Billy Wayne's abandoned Lincoln were suspicious enough by themselves, but he reminded himself to leave Esco in the car for the rest of the day. He himself had on his finest linen and silk jacket, his most perfectly faded blue jeans, and an expensive polo shirt. But he suspected the effect was lost on the deputy, who wouldn't know taste from tinsel. The deputy made a phone call, gave someone named Sammy directions, asked him to check on the registration, and waited, the phone to his ear and his fingers drumming on the desktop. After a moment he began to say, "Yep . . . yep . . . yep," into the phone, read some numbers into it from the title he held before him, and then said, "yep . . . yep," again until he hung up. "So," he said, sighing and leaning back in his chair to look from one of them to the other, "you fellers tell me the car wasn't stolen and nobody wants to press any charges."

"Mr. Roland already told you that, didn't he?" Jerry said. "Hell, I just came to get it."

"He never told me a thing, for I never talked to him," the deputy said. "I wasn't here when they traced down the tags and called him. Okay," he said, "I'll need your signature and forty-five dollars, and I'll give you directions to the town garage and a release so you can pick her up."

"What for?" Jerry said.

"What for, what?" the deputy said.

"The forty-five dollars?" Jerry said.

"Well, twenty-five is for towing charges," the deputy said.

"What's the other twenty?" Jerry said.

The deputy sucked an eyetooth. "Paperwork."

Jerry decided not to ask him where the car had been found; the man was simply too testy and suspicious to deal with. Probably, like most police, he had his own scam going.

"Now if the car had been stolen, I expect the insurance company would be right tickled to pay forty-five dollars instead of fifteen or twenty thousand or whatever that thing cost."

"Jesus," Jerry said. He wasn't so sure how easy it would be to get his money back from Billy Wayne. He got out his billfold, thumbed through its contents, and flipped two twenties and a ten on the counter. While the deputy scribbled on a form, Jerry fingered the money he had left, biliousness creeping toward his eyes.

Esco chuckled, which made Jerry furious. Chances were that Esco wasn't laughing because of the forty-five dollars. Chances were Esco understood very little of what was going on. He wasn't smart, and anything he didn't understand seemed to amuse him—likely because, since he seldom saw the logic behind a situation it seemed, by definition, senseless and silly. Esco was amused a lot. Only those few things he did understand had the power to make him grave.

"Where did you find Mr. Roland's car at?" Esco said.

"Out on the Cove Creek Pike," the deputy said, "sittin beside the road pretty as you please with the keys in the ignition." He slid a form to Jerry, pointed where he wanted it signed, and handed the pen to him. "You'll want to take a can of gas with you. There doesn't seem to be a thing wrong with it, except it's got an empty tank."

"Haven't seen anything of a strange blond-headed chick around, have you?" Esco said.

"Nope," the deputy said.

Luckily, Jerry thought, the deputy was busy giving him his change, a receipt, and a release, and so wasn't paying much attention to Esco.

"Well . . ." Esco said.

"Shut up and let him tell us where to get the car, for Christ's sake, will you?" Jerry said and gave him a hard warning glance.

Esco smiled and shrugged.

When they were outside the courthouse and about to get in their red Camaro, nosed in between a police car and a dusty pickup, Jerry said, "What in hell did you bring up the girl for?" Esco's forehead wrinkled in puzzlement, but the silly smile remained on his face, something like the smile on the face of an infant who was passing gas. Esco merely shrugged. "Get in the car!" Jerry said, and when they were both inside, Jerry studied him and shook his head. "If he'd asked what her name was, you would have told him, wouldn't you? You'd have smiled that shit-eating grin and told him!"

Esco could feel something between his cheeks at that very moment, and he suspected it was a shit-eating grin, but he couldn't help it. It was merely the expression his face settled into all on its own. He couldn't see what all the fuss was about.

"What if we find that bitch and have to strangle her? You go asking the goddamned fuzz about Sally Ann Shaw, who do you think they're gonna look for when her dead body turns up? Huh? You dipstick!"

Esco frowned. He hadn't thought about strangling Sally. "How we gonna find her if we don't ask folks if they've seen her?" he said.

"Back this thing up and go down South Main on the other side of the square," Jerry said. It was, of course, a perfectly good question. His own feeling, however, was that they had a piss poor chance of ever seeing her again. And of course they would have to ask around, and that meant if they found her and had to kill her, they'd have to make sure her body never turned up, which meant hiding it where it couldn't be found, or destroying it so that it did not exist to be found.

"Huh?" Esco said.

It was an interesting problem. "Shut up," Jerry told him. "Look for Locust Street and turn left when you find it."

At the garage Jerry talked to a black fellow named Sammy who ran the tow truck and who explained exactly where Roland's car had been abandoned. Jerry described Sally Ann Shaw to him, claiming to be her brother, claiming that Sally and Roland were married and had had a fight, and she had run off in the car. He thought he'd used just the right tone, just the right mixture of brotherly concern and humor over the shenanigans of women, but the black didn't know anything. Still, it was a pretty good story, and he decided to stick to it when he made inquiries at the bus station and at the local taxi stand. He gave Sammy a five-dollar bill for his trouble and Sammy found him a short piece of rope to tow the Lincoln to a gas station. It was his notion that you could have a laugh or two with a black, slip him a few bucks, and he wouldn't give you away. Hell, they wouldn't tell the fuzz much of anything any time, just as a matter of principle. They were a damned close-mouthed race; he'd give them that.

He put Esco behind the wheel of the Lincoln, dropped him at a Shell station, and said he'd meet him in an hour at a Big John's Barbecue they'd passed on the way into town. Esco was smiling like a Buddha behind the wheel of the enormous Lincoln since he hadn't yet realized he was about to be stuck for twenty-five or thirty dollars worth of lead-free premium.

Finding the bus station was an easy matter, and the woman at the ticket counter was helpful. She had grown altogether damp-eyed when he told his story in which Roland had become a wife beater; Sally Ann had acquired a drinking habit; and he, himself, had become the concerned brother who was always pulling her out of one jam or another, who had already gone to the police and received no help and didn't know where else to turn. She telephoned the man who worked the third shift, and Jerry talked to him; but Sally Ann Shaw had caught no bus out of that town, at least not in the early morning hours of the night she'd taken Roland's car and money. The woman squeezed his arm, wished him luck, and called him "honey" when he left.

The taxi stand only kept four cars on the street and only one from the hours of two to five-thirty in the morning. He got to talk to the cabby who'd had the shift, a scruffy little man no bigger than a jockey who dribbled ashes from his cigarette down his shirtfront and claimed to have picked up no blondes that night, drunken, beaten up, or otherwise. The cab stand was a seedy place, not much more than a hole in the wall with a telephone and a radio for the dispatcher and a broken-down couch for sleeping as much as sitting, if one could judge by the stained pillow without a pillowcase and the grubby blanket trailing from the couch to the floor. Jerry did not trust either the cabby or the dispatcher. The fetor of stale cigarettes and dirty underwear tainted the air of the tiny office, and Jerry felt that fifty dollars would easily have bought the silence of anyone there. Hell, a few thousand would probably have bought the whole operation, and Sally Ann had a quarter of a million. The seedy little cabby could easily have driven her to some place in town or taken her all the way to Atlanta. Jerry's touching story clearly didn't move them at all, and he decided, if nothing else turned up in the towns nearby, he'd get Esco to bend the driver a little. Esco would enjoy it, whether or not the driver was telling the truth; anyway, it was what the unsympathetic little son of a bitch deserved.

He found Esco at Big John's eating barbecue and getting grease spots on his leisure suit. He had a barbecue himself and tried to decide if he should bother to look over the place where the Lincoln had been found. If there was a house close by, it was possible someone could have seen her stop; seen her walk on toward town, or back toward the interstate highway, or get into a familiar car. And what if she'd holed up nearby? What if she'd hidden the briefcase within twenty-five or thirty yards of where the Lincoln quit, so as not to be encumbered by it? Christ, there were at least a dozen reasons to take a look around.

But say she'd merely walked back to the interstate and stuck out her thumb? She'd be gone without a trace. Hell, that's what he would have done. No, he thought, no he wouldn't, because he wouldn't have been dumb enough to run out of gas in the first place. Likely she'd noticed she was about to run out and had turned off the interstate to find a station and simply had the poor luck to run dry before she found anything. What if someone had picked her up, cut her silly throat, and kept the money for himself. That was possible. With the riffraff and scum around these days, it was more than possible.

When Esco had finished his fourth large barbecue sandwich, he dabbed at his lips with a napkin and sighed happily. "You don't put enough hot sauce on em," he told Jerry. "And slaw," he said, "they ain't no good without slaw and hot sauce on em."

"I should have had a goddamned milkshake," Jerry said and grimaced in anticipation of the indigestion he would surely suffer for thinking he could eat what Esco ate and get away with it.

"You find out anything?" Esco asked.

"Nobody's seen her," Jerry said, "but those bastards at the taxi stand might be lying. If we don't turn up any leads in the next day or so, you might need to shake a little truth out of a cabby."

"Sure," Esco said, rubbing at some barbecue sauce he had discovered on his shirt. It didn't come off very well, so he dampened his napkin on his tongue and tried again. He knew it was not wise to admit it, but he was entertained. The stolen car and money; Roland's concussion, he wasn't quite certain just what a concussion was; the glass in Roland's penis, he couldn't figure how in the world it had gotten in there; and trying to find Sally, who had done these things to Roland—all that was exciting and made a nice change from being a bouncer in Roland's club. He especially liked the idea that he might have to make someone tell the truth. He hoped they wouldn't find out anything, and he would have to make the cabby tell them what they wanted to know. He knew he could do it. Ever since he was quite young, he had been good at making people say whatever he wanted them to. He simply caught hold of them and bent their arms or their necks, or squeezed some part of their bodies, and he could win any argument. It had been a valuable thing to learn, and it had given him great peace and contentment. Before he learned it, he had been tormented by people who thought they were smarter than he was, but once they found out his strength, they quit bothering him. Oh, a few would always try to make him look stupid and then run away. They knew they had to run since he could make them eat dirt and take everything back and look even dumber than they had tried to make him look. It didn't bother him that they would say nasty things and run; he knew how it would turn out. He never chased them because he couldn't catch them; but, sometime or other, he'd get them unawares and make them take it all back and more to boot. It had made him a very peaceful person, and he almost never had to use his strength anymore, even as a bouncer. Usually all he had to do was show himself and ask one or two people to leave. It was rare when he actually had to take hold of someone and help them leave. Insults didn't even bother him anymore, and he didn't have to make a person take them back; just knowing he could was enough to make him happy. Anyway, few people insulted him these days except Roland, once in a while, and Jerry, but it didn't bother him because he could even make them eat dirt if he wanted to. He was a very happy person. Happier than Roland. Happier than Jerry, who was nervous and had a bad stomach. He wasn't even going to eat all of his sandwich, Esco could tell. Jerry had made a face and pushed the barbecue away from him. Jerry wasn't very healthy.

"I guess we ought to leave that goddamned Lincoln here; it might make the police wonder if they happened to see it parked back where they just picked it up."

Esco wasn't sure whether Jerry was talking to him or merely thinking out loud. "Don't you want the rest of that barbecue?" he said.

Jerry shook his head, belched, and made a disagreeable face. "Come on, for Christ's sake," he said.

But Esco opened the barbecue, shook some hot sauce on it, emptied the little paper cup of slaw over it, and ate the whole thing in one bite. Jerry had paid for it. It was dumb to just leave it there. He emptied the paper plates and trash from their table into a built-in container that said *Thank You* on its swinging door and caught up with Jerry just as he was about to get in the Camaro. Jerry pitched him the keys across the roof.

"Head out of town and turn right when you see a sign to the Cove Creek Pike," Jerry told him. And later when they were on the proper road, he said, "It was supposed to be just this side of a curve sign about two miles out."

When they found the place and had pulled over, Esco said, "What do you expect to find anyhow?"

"Nothing," Jerry said. "I don't expect to find a goddamned thing, so I don't guess I'll be disappointed." He got out of the car and looked around. It was the proper spot all right; the Lincoln had sat on the shoulder long enough to sink into the ground a little, and he could see where the wrecker had backed around; but there wasn't a house anywhere in sight. Still, he thought he ought to inquire at the first couple of houses in either direction and tell his little story about his sister. His notion that she might have hidden the briefcase somewhere close to keep from looking so conspicuous with it, or merely to disencumber herself, seemed more and more unlikely, but having admitted it as a possibility, it would gnaw at him if he didn't check it out. "Let's scout around a little bit," he told Esco.

"Why?" Esco said. "What are we lookin for?"

"A quarter of a million bucks in a briefcase, goddamn it. She might have hid it when she ran out of gas. A punched-out chippy beside the road at three in the morning is one thing," Jerry said, "but give her a fancy briefcase, and you might think a whole different way, right?"

Esco merely grinned and shrugged.

On the far side of the road there was a four-foot cut with a fence and a rocky pasture just beyond it. Jerry checked it out and found no more than he expected; there wasn't any cover on the high side of the road, but on Esco's side there was a jungle of woods, waist-high grass, and feathery thickets of cane. It seemed a waste of time, but he went over to look with Esco, who was off to the left moving around in the thick growth like a bear. He himself hadn't even stepped off the shoulder when he noticed the faint trail of bent grasses and cane. "Did you do this?" he called to Esco.

"Do what? I ain't got down that far yet," Esco said.

It could have been nothing at all, or it could have been an animal, but it looked to Jerry as if something had passed through there, going, more or less, straight away from the road. He stepped across the ditch and followed. About thirty yards from the road he came to spongy, damp ground. He had been looking carefully for tracks, but had found none, at least none he was sure of, and once or twice he thought he'd even lost the faint trail he was following; but then, right in front of him, was a clear print, not of a foot, but a hand. "Well goddamn," he whispered, and knelt to study it. He put his own hand out to cover it. She fell, he thought. She came through here, and she fell. He was still squatting on his heels and staring at the small, perfect print of her hand when Esco came blundering up behind him; but he had seen other marks by that time, too, as though finding the print of her hand had somehow snapped his eyes into focus, mysteriously improved his vision. He had found the much lighter print of her left hand beside the right one. He had found the deep indentation of the sharp heels of her shoes, a mark he'd seen three or four times before but hadn't recognized. When Esco reached him he stood up and carefully took off his linen jacket, delicately shook it out, and handed it to him. "Take it back to the car for me," he said. "You might as well shed your own too. That silly bitch came through here," he said. "God knows where she thinks she's going. Be careful with that," he said, flipping his forefinger at his jacket, "and lock the damn car."

Slowly, carefully, but not without losing her trail three or four times, they followed her all the way to the river, where they stood puzzling over the skid marks on the bank; apparently, she had entered the water.

"Maybe she drown," Esco said, his cheeks red and glistening and his purple shirt black with sweat.

"Maybe," Jerry said.

"Or maybe she swum across," Esco said, looking at the far shore nearly a hundred yards away. "Jesus."

"Maybe," Jerry said. He had been feeling smart and slick as hell. He'd half-expected to find her, perhaps dead, perhaps hiding. And certainly he'd had a little luck, but he'd made the luck. No big city detective could have done better. And now this. It didn't make any sense. No sense at all. "You go up the bank," he told Esco, "and see if you can find any place where she came out of the water and I'll go down." It didn't wash that she'd steal the car and the money and then drown herself, but he supposed she might have done it. Maybe, after all, some crazy fit had come over her. It made more sense than to think she'd try to swim the river. There was nothing over there he could see except woods. He had the feeling he was surrounded by idiots, Sally Ann and Esco no less than Billy Wayne; sure Billy Wayne had him a fancy club on Printer's Alley, and half the big shots in country music called him any time they wanted to feel happy or to get up for a performance, or get down from one, or mellow out—hell, they couldn't do without him. But how seriously could you take him when he'd let some cheap bitch steal more than two hundred thousand and his car, and leave him with a knot on his head the size of a baseball and a mangled cock. Christ, the surgeon had had to slit the skin on it and peel it back like a sock, then cut the son of a bitch all the way open to get the glass out, and then stitch the whole mess back together so that now Roland's prick looked like a blood sausage somebody had hit with a hammer. Well, it was no more than he deserved. Roland puffed himself up like some big-time gangster or hotshot producer, but he wasn't so much. He wasn't even very smart. He had no style. Hell, he dressed like a nigger pimp, Jerry told himself and laughed, but his laughter grew bitter when he realized that he, Jerry, was merely Roland's delivery boy and was paid very little more than Esco, who wasn't any smarter than the average Doberman pinscher. He promised himself if he got the money back, he'd ask for a raise, no, a percentage, and maybe a finder's fee to boot. Of course if Roland had any class at all, he wouldn't even have to ask.

After he'd covered nearly five hundred yards of riverbank and nearly ruined a pair of loafers that had cost him a hundred and a quarter, he went back up the river to find Esco and saw something he hadn't seen before. Twenty feet straight out from where Sally Ann had apparently gone into the river there was a piece of twine slanting down from a low branch into the water. It wasn't very noticeable, but it was there, and it was obviously under tension. When Esco came back, Jerry made him take off his pants and wade out to investigate, but the twine turned out to have hooks on it baited with small fish. "Sure," Esco said, "it's only a trotline somebody's set. Some dumb fisherman."

# 7

A little before six in the evening he came downriver, the long, smooth glide of his johnboat reined in and made sluggish by the insides of two minnow buckets he was dragging from the stern like sea anchors. Still, he was in no particular hurry to get home; it made his palms misty just to think about it. Before the girl arrived, coming back to his camp had been like putting on an old shirt, since the spirit of his habitation, and none other, dwelt in all its spaces. But he could sense her presence the moment he came in sight of his boats tethered to the shore. Nothing had changed, but somehow, it all looked different, the boats, the leggy vegetables growing in the dappled shade of his garden, and the tree house itself, which he could glimpse now and again through the leaves of maple and oak, sycamore and willow. Yet he'd had little enough to do with her. For days, in fact, they had been skirting one another, polite, awkward, distant, careful even to avoid each other's eyes. He'd gotten friendlier with women he'd sat next to on a bus; but, of course, that made sense; a bus was a bus, and a tree house was another thing altogether. In a tree house there was way the hell more privacy than he knew what to do with and no rules at all.

Even though he took his time, he got there anyway, nosed the johnboat up on the muddy little spit of sand beside the others, and pitched out his anchor in case the river should rise. He transferred his minnows to the live trap he kept in his holding pool; and, as though he were putting off climbing up into the tree house as long as he could, he took a peck bucket and went to his garden where he dug some new potatoes, pulled some onions, and gathered lettuce, cucumbers, and tomatoes. Kneeling by the stream of water that ran from the overflow pipe of his springhouse, he washed the potatoes and onions carefully. Then he washed his hands and face and combed his fingers through his hair and beard. Finally he dried his hands, front and back, on the thighs of his trousers; and, thus composed, picked up his bucket of vegetables, climbed the ladder, and entered his tree house. But he wasn't prepared at all for the new woman she had become.

"Hi there!" she said, all freshly scrubbed and smiling and full of a kind of cheery domesticity that surrounded her like perfume. "Did you catch lots of fish?"

There weren't any shoes on her feet and her face was as innocent of makeup as an apple he might have polished on his sleeve, but she was wearing a satiny yellow dress fancy enough for a party. "I was after bait," Toots managed to say at last.

"Well, did you get lots of bait then?" she asked him.

He only half heard her. He was looking around at how clean and tidy the camp was. Somehow it was far neater than it had ever been before, but from the gouges in the floor where raw wood showed a number of recent woundings, it looked as if she'd gone after the dirt with a hoe as well as a broom. He'd forgotten what she asked him, but he didn't think it mattered; he'd sensed many times before that women were capable of asking all sorts of questions when they were supremely uninterested in the answers.

"I'm just feeling a whole lot better than I did for a while," she said. "You've been real sweet, but I don't want you waiting on me hand and foot. Anyway, it's high time I did some of the cooking around here for a change."

He blinked at her, taken aback.

"What'cha got in the bucket?" she said, took it from him, and peered inside. "Oh, what pretty vegetables. So," she said and smiled brightly at him, "what's on the menu?"

He cleared his throat and found a voice, although it was not his own. He told her what he thought they'd have for supper, but insisted on doing the cooking himself. "It's right hard to cook on a camp stove if you're not used to it," he told her.

"Well," she said, "I'm going to help and that's that, and I can start by making the salad."

If there was a way to deny her, he couldn't think of it, and he climbed down out of the tree house as much to get away from her and collect his wits as to net a catfish from his holding pool and dress it out. What had come over her all of a sudden, he wondered. He dipped up a fine channel cat and nailed its whiskered head to a tree. She'd made up her mind about something, he was sure of that. He tried to be reasonable; he even laughed a little at himself, although it was a miserable, breathy sort of laughter. What could she want, after all, with a ragged, one-eyed hermit who was old enough to be her grandfather? He slit the skin just behind the catfish's head, and, after two or three failed attempts, pulled the skin from the fish's body with a pair of pliers. He was running his knife down the backbone to fillet it when she came out along the catwalk to fetch water from the mossy pipe driven into the bluff. He couldn't think what she reminded him of with her bare feet and her slender legs flashing beneath the satiny, yellow dress.

Up in the tree house with her a few moments before, he'd noticed that her bad eye had begun to open up again, and, what with the puffiness of her lip going down, it was possible to see what she had looked like before she'd been beaten. She had been pretty and was about to be again. Not beautiful like models in magazines, not a girl who would turn heads; perhaps no better favored than girls one might see on thousands of street corners in thousands of towns, who would have the power to break a heart only if a fellow paused long enough to see the subtle and individual qualities not noticeable at a glance. Her wide-set eyes, for example, with the motes of light in their depths. The curve of her high cheekbones. The barest hint of a cleft in her chin, neither clearly vulnerable nor defiant.

He was burying the ravaged skeleton of the catfish in his garden—the gill flaps still lifting occasionally, the whiskered mouth, now and again, taking a gulp of air—when she came out a second time, all friendliness and cheer. "Hey down there!" she called, "where in the world do you keep your vinegar?"

It was none of her business where he kept his vinegar, and he had an impulse to tell her so, but he told her it was behind the coffee can on the second shelf.

He had decided to make cornbread, but it took an unmercifully long time to bake in the little portable tin oven set atop the camp stove, and even the new potatoes, half the size of hen's eggs though most of them were, didn't want to get done. And all the while she bustled about, smiling, friendly, helpful. He tried, grimly, to keep his mind on cooking, watching things that didn't need to be watched, poking things that had already been poked to pieces. She set the table, put down folded paper towels to serve as napkins; and when at last the cornbread and potatoes were done, she set them out on plates, rather than leaving the cornbread in the pie tin and the potatoes in the pot as he would have. He didn't know whether he was relieved or not when the catfish was finally brown and ready. But he served her plate and his own directly from the frying pan and sat down determined to fill his mouth with food in order to absolve himself of the responsibility of conversation, which he hadn't made anyway except for the abrupt answers he gave her when she asked where something was kept.

"Mmmmh," she said after her first bite of fish, "delicious."

"Eat then," he said, "before it gets cold."

But she was clearly in a mood to talk, and with a dreamy, half-humorous light in her eye, she told about a fellow she had lived with in Huntsville, Alabama, before she decided to trot off to Nashville with her silly notion of trying to break into the country music business. He'd operated a bulldozer, she told him, and was tall and nice looking and had loved to party and have a good time. But she'd just up and left him one day while he was at work, even though he hadn't been mean to her at all. She still missed him at odd moments, she said, because he had such a good disposition and such nice teeth and was a terrific dancer.

Toots poked a potato in his mouth and motioned with his fork for her to do the same, but she only probed her food absentmindedly.

Before she'd lived with the fellow in Huntsville, she told Toots, she had been a waitress in half a dozen places, lived briefly with another man, worked in a grocery store, in a cotton mill, and had even been a go-go dancer. She had been on her own, she said, since she was sixteen when she'd run off from her family. She shook her head and gave a tiny, halfhearted snort of laughter. "My momma and daddy were good, decent people," she said. "There wasn't any way they deserved the grief I caused them. Ha, sometimes even on purpose, as though I was trying to get back at them for something they'd done to me, when they hadn't done anything at all." She shook her head again and smiled, as though she wanted what she told him to be merely funny, and explained how, some way or other, she thought she'd been born with her hackles up, already out of patience about something. She wasn't sure just what—being born poor maybe, being born a girl, being born in some out of the way, jerkwater town in Alabama. But whatever it was, she had been testy about it ever since she was a little girl in grade school; and as a consequence, she'd been ready to try out anything rumored to be exciting, particularly if it was going to go against the grain of her parents and that dull little town. And so she had been the first girl she knew to taste alcohol, to smoke pot, to have sex, and, ultimately, to leave home. But all of it, she told him, had been a disappointment.

"I guess I convinced everyone, even my momma and daddy, that I was a bad girl, but I never did feel bad; I mean I never did set out to hurt anybody," she said and peered earnestly across the table at him as though she expected him to confirm her innocence.

He tried to think of something to say to absolve her, but before he could even make a consoling gesture, she seemed to have forgotten about him and was merely staring into the space between them. Her eyes began to grow a little damp, and her chin crinkled bitterly. "Ha," she said, "I just had the awful thought that maybe people who are mean don't feel mean, even the worst of them. Maybe only good people feel mean. Jesus, what do you think?"

"I don't know," he said. She seemed to ponder a moment, and in that brief space of quiet he could hear a cicada winding down in a tree close by and, somewhere away, a mourning dove make its forlorn, four-noted comment.

"Well anyway," she said, "I never felt mean. I felt stubborn; I admit to that. Ever since I was a tiny child, I've felt stubborn and sometimes very brave; although I guess I'd be better off if I wasn't either one since they seemed to get me into a lot more trouble than they ever got me out of. Being brave would just come over me whether I wanted it or needed it or didn't. It's a funny feeling," she told him, "all airy and light-headed, and it tastes almost sweet in your mouth when it comes. But the stubbornness, now, that's something else again. It feels heavy and tastes as dull and bitter as brass. I just always, you know, wanted to be something special, somebody grand, and I just couldn't wait. I just . . ." All at once her eyes seemed to snap into focus, and she was looking at him almost as if she were surprised to find him still sitting across the table from her, and she blushed. "Phooey," she said.

He had no notion what he was supposed to do or say. He'd never been any good at figuring out his responsibilities to a conversation, and as often as not, he got in over his head when he tried. "Your dinner's gonna get cold," he told her. "Eat. It'll make you strong."

"No," she said, "not until I tell you what I'm trying to tell you." Her eyes were brimming with tears, and she let out a little bark of laughter. "I just can't seem to get it said."

"Don't tell me anything," he said. "Eat. Eat."

"I don't know whether I'm scared or mad," she said. "I didn't want his stupid money or his car. A week ago I could walk down the street like anybody, get my hair fixed, go to a movie, make all sorts of plans, and now I've got to hide from some puffed-up asshole who thinks he's God. He thought he could treat me any damned way he wanted, as if I wasn't anything at all. Well," she said, her eyes dazzled with tears, "well sir, I may be a little screwed up, but somewhere you can bet Mr. Billy Wayne Roland is holding his cock and gritting his teeth. Yes, sir, and you can bet Sally Ann Shaw will turn out to be the most expensive piece of ass he'll ever have. Ha," she said and wiped each eye with a single angry swipe and blew her nose on the paper towel she'd put beside her plate.

He struggled to swallow a piece of fish that went down, at last, like a wad of tinfoil. Why, he wondered, did women have to be so excitable? Apparently she was jealous because someone named Sally had run off with her boyfriend; he couldn't quite get the drift of the rest of it, but he could see she was upset. "Don't cry," he told her.

"I'm not crying," she insisted, glaring at him through brimming eyes.

"Everything will turn out all right," he told her.

"Sure," she said. She got up and yanked her laundry bag from beneath the cot. "Hey, since the son of a bitch beat me and raped me just more or less for fun, and since I only bashed him on the head and stole about a zillion dollars and his fancy new car from him," she said and began to shake out endless, tumbled stacks of bills among the colorful silk and lace of slips and underthings, "and, hey, since I left him about half dead and with his pecker full of broken glass, I don't see why we can't just call . . ."

"Wait," Toots said. "Wait." He was so confused, it took him some time to think of a question to ask. "Who is Sally Ann Shaw?" he said at last.

But it didn't seem to do her any good to tell him. She had to go over the whole thing again while his blue eye grew round and blinked like the shutter of a camera, and he cried "wait, wait," and asked one question after another.

# 8

"Just because you saved my life once," she said, "you don't have to keep on doing it."

Oddly, explaining things again and again had turned her dry-eyed and resigned; but Toots paced back and forth tugging on the top of one ear as though he meant to pull it from the side of his head.

"You being so nice and all, I figured I owed you the truth," she told him. "Anyway I couldn't hold it inside anymore. I wouldn't blame you if you turned me out," she said.

"What if you sent his money back?" Toots said.

Her stomach betrayed the thought almost before she could consider it, as though the very center of her remembered with utter clarity the absolute cruelty of the rape, a cruelty that not only would not have abated at the point of her death, but seemed to seek it as its final sexual pleasure. Somehow her stomach told her that Billy Wayne Roland would want her dead if only because she had survived to defy him. She could give back anything she wanted, and it wouldn't change what she had done. When he'd cursed her, she'd cursed him back. When he'd hit her, she'd hit him back. And when he had raped her, she'd bashed him, taken his fancy car, his money, stuck a thermometer in him and smashed it to smithereens. And as crazy as it sounded, she promised herself that when he killed her, if she could contrive, somehow, to do it, she'd kill him back, by Jesus.

"Huh?" Toots said. "What if you sent his money back to him?" He pulled the tip of his ear while she sat before her uneaten food, her shoulders drooping and her head hung. "I'll take it to him," he said. "Hell, and his car too."

She merely looked at her plate, and he thought for a moment she might agree. Absently she wiped her upper lip, still damp from weeping. "I'd burn it first," she said.

Toots blinked at her and let go of his ear, which was getting tender where it was anchored to his head. "Okay," he said, "all right." He sat down across from her in the dim evening light to think things over. After a while he got up again and lit two kerosene lamps and stood for a moment with his hands in his pockets. "Tell me again where you left his car?"

"I don't know," she said. "It wasn't more than a mile or so off the interstate. It's not very far. That way, I think," she said and tipped her head toward the southwest.

"And you left the keys in it?"

"Yes," she said.

"Did anybody see you after it stopped running?"

"I didn't see anybody until I saw you," she said.

He crossed the room, rummaged under the sideboard, and pulled out two cans of Coleman fuel. One was unopened. He shook the other and guessed it was nearly half full. "I don't see why it won't run on this," he said. He stood for a moment looking about, as though he was suddenly at a loss to understand how his life had gotten so complicated. He considered the enormous pile of twenty-dollar bills and her lacy underthings like small, showy creatures who had expired helter-skelter among them; and he considered her, her yellow dress, the marks of the beating her face still bore, her upper lip still damp from weeping. He took a huge breath and let it whistle out through his nose.

"What are you going to do?" she said.

"I'm going to move that car," he said.

"But it's getting dark. Hey, I don't think I much want to be here by myself in the dark," she said and tried to laugh.

"Nobody's going to be stumbling around this bluff at night," he said.

"I can shoot a gun," she said. "My father showed me when I was little. Maybe you've got a gun I could have just until you get back." She laughed nervously, shaking all the while as though she were cold. "If you could load it and explain just a little . . ."

He shook his head. "I don't have a gun," he said. Somehow he'd lost interest in them after he'd come out of the army; he didn't even know what had become of the guns he'd once owned. Without a right eye, he would have had to teach himself to shoot left-handed, and it hadn't seemed worth the trouble. "You don't need a gun," he said. "When I leave, pull the ladder up. It would take a squirrel to get up here then."

She wiped her upper lip again. "Can't you wait till in the morning?" she said.

"I expect we've waited too long already," he said.

But when he climbed down with his cans of fuel, he found that she was unable to retrieve the ladder, and he had to climb into the tree house again and pull it up himself. He laid the ladder along the catwalk and decided to let himself down through the trap door. He hooked his rope and tackle to the heavy eye bolt in his roof beam and opened the trap door. "I'll drive the car down the interstate as far as it will run," he said, "so I might not get back till nearly daylight." He rubbed the palms of his hands on his thighs as though that were some mysterious preparation for climbing down the rope. "I'll give a holler and you can open up and drop the rope down to me."

She wiped her fingertips over her upper lip again, which seemed to be perpetually dewy ever since her confession. "You don't have to do this," she said and gave him a long and searching look while he tried to decide if he did or if he didn't, but there seemed to be no proper test for the answer. Without taking her eyes from his face, she shook her head sadly and smiled a shaky, embarrassed smile. "Hey," she said, "if I ever had a lucky day, it was when I met you," and without any warning, she hugged him, pinning his arms to his sides and squeezing him fiercely. He could feel her heart beat and a slow steady trembling that seemed to shake all of her, even the crown of her head tucked under his chin. At least he thought the trembling had been hers, but when she released him and he slid down the rope, he discovered his body still retained it, so perhaps it had been his all along.

Once on the ground he satisfied himself that it would be very hard for anyone to climb up to her while he was gone. Even if someone were able to shinny up the trees, the floor of the tree house would stop them, and the catwalks were so wide, no one could reach the edges to gain a purchase there. Even his old route up the bluff to the mouth of the cave was blocked by the floor of the tree house. No, he thought, unless someone brought their own ladder, or a rope and a grappling hook, there was little chance of getting to her.

He gathered up his cans of fuel and went on down the floodplain toward the southern end of the bluff where the climbing was not so difficult. He'd gone a hundred and fifty yards before he realized he'd been too distracted to think of bringing a flashlight, but the night was going to be clear and moony, and he only paused a moment before he decided he could get along without and went on. By the time he reached the top of the bluff, it was full dark, the whippoorwills had struck up, and the pale moon was riding above the scrub oak and stunted pine.

No one had yet built along the top of the bluff, not even Louise, but down closer to the Bear Creek Pike there were half a dozen elegant houses, each on its groomed five-acre plot. Like a ragged hobgoblin in the faint polish of the moonlight, he passed them by, his black basketball shoes hissing softly on the curving plane of the street. Behind one of the grand houses a dog barked uncertainly and not long, a big dog by the sound of it, but it did not appear. There were no streetlights, but the houses themselves often had lamps along their driveways or walks, or on their porches or patios, as well as lights within, which gleamed through windows to dwell on thoroughly domesticated shrubs, so that each house existed inside the sparkling nimbus of its own illumination. Somehow the neighborhood was so prosperous and sedate it seemed unimaginable that just over the bluff his rude shelter was perched in the trees or that someone like Sally Ann Shaw was hiding there. No one was going to find her, he thought, car or no car.

When he came to the Bear Creek Pike, he turned left toward Clifton, wondering if the Lincoln was even going to be there. An old Ford or a Chevy or a pickup truck might remain parked on the shoulder of the road for a week, or even longer, without arousing anyone's curiosity, or even so much as a second glance. Anyone who even bothered to notice such a vehicle would figure a broken fuel pump, or a blown head gasket, or a leaky radiator hose had forced some poor bastard to abandon it, and sooner or later he'd come back to tow it away or lean under the open hood to curse and strain until, ultimately, he got it going again. But not so with such a grand, showy automobile as she described. The police wouldn't pass it more than twice before they stopped to investigate, since the wealthy simply didn't abandon their cars beside the road. It was possible too that some local punk had spotted the car and found it irresistible, having the keys in the ignition, as it did, and not a single thing wrong with it except a gas gauge that read empty. Still, if it was there, he'd turn it around and drive it down the interstate toward Atlanta as far as it would go. He'd take the Coleman cans with him, he decided, and hide them on the way back, miles from where he left the car.

But he never asked himself what he proposed to do with the girl or with the unaccountable giddiness that buzzed in his bones; it was a feeling he hadn't had since his youth, a ludicrous feeling he had no intention of acknowledging. He kept on down the road, squinting, as he rounded each curve, to catch sight of the yellow Lincoln.

When he'd slid down the rope and left her, she'd been frightened. She pulled the rope up, shut the trap door, and tried to watch him through the window that looked south down the river, but the soft lamplight inside the camp caused the window to give back only her own ghostly reflection. She felt cold even though the night was balmy, and she worried that Billy Wayne just might be outside somewhere, lurking in deep shadows, watching Toots leave. First she stuffed the money and her underthings into the laundry bag and shoved it under her bunk, but then she stood for a long moment hugging herself and fighting a strong impulse to run out on the catwalk and call Toots back. Yet she did not for fear she had already waited too long. If she were to call and Toots didn't answer, she knew the silence would terrify her. Instead she took one of his long-sleeved shirts from a nail along the wall and put it on. It smelled faintly of sweat and something else, the woods perhaps, or the riverbank, but the odor was not unpleasant, merely rather human and male and somewhat comforting. Not knowing what else to do, she sat down at the table and hugged herself again. No doubt Toots was right, she told herself, and nobody was going to be stumbling around out there in the dark. And she couldn't see how they could get up into the tree house even if they were. But she preferred to believe they weren't there at all. She had no wish to test their ingenuity; she didn't like to think about them watching her through one of the small windows, or even listening to her footsteps cross and recross the floor.

She sat at the table a long time before she began to feel mysteriously better. She'd told Toots everything—she hadn't planned to be quite so damned honest, but somehow she'd got off to an odd start and there hadn't seemed to be any good place or any good reason to stop—and he hadn't thrown her out. She couldn't believe she'd told him about her childhood, or that she had actually dumped all that money out for him to see. She'd told him things she hadn't quite known about herself, but now she had an ally. Maybe, she thought, just maybe, in some mysterious way, the closest ally she'd ever had. She felt vastly relieved, somehow buoyant and free, if a tiny bit guilty about the way she'd acted. She didn't think she'd said anything that wasn't true, but somehow she knew her behavior hadn't been quite so honest, although it was a dishonesty she'd practiced ever since she'd been a small girl, a kind of seductive sweetness that had always been rewarded. Still, she felt she was less guilty of such behavior than almost any girl she'd ever met. In fact, she told herself, the difference between her and the good girls was that the good girls acted that way all the time, until they believed it, until it became what they were. She felt virtuous by comparison and smiled to herself, rubbing the palms of her hands up and down her arms. "Yes," she said, speaking softly but aloud to herself, "and you don't sing worth a shit either."

She didn't know where the admission had come from or what had provoked her to make it. But there it was. She had spoken it aloud, and even while some part of her tried to backwater, tried to insist that she carried a tune well enough, that her voice was pleasing, and that there were others with no more talent who had gotten all the things she wanted, she admitted the truth of it. She was astonished and a bit dazed, but she could feel, as though magically, another weight beginning to lift, the awful, dull weight of false ambition, of unfulfilled and unattainable aspiration that somehow had outgrown the daydream, the thin fancy of some otherwise unremarkable afternoon until it had become a religion that sustained her and stayed with her even after the rituals turned hollow and the God false.

May Morning was a name for a little girl to give one of her dolls, but not herself. It was a ghastly truth to recognize, but if Toots had been there, she suspected she would have confessed these things too. Maybe, she thought, Billy Wayne *had* killed her; for certain she felt strangely empty and utterly new. She was a whole new person who happened to have a hell of a lot of money and also a friend. "When you come back," she told Toots, "I'm gonna squeeze you half to death. I'm gonna hug you till you holler."

Rubbing the palms of her hands up and down her arms

as though she were warming up to do just that, she noticed the dinner he had cooked for her. It was stone cold, but she took up her fork and had a bite of fish. It was a tentative, experimental bite, but the fish tasted remarkably good. To her surprise, she found that she was quite hungry and hadn't any trouble eating everything on her plate, cold as it was. With a touch of shame, she took a large second helping of salad and potatoes and ate that too.

She would have liked to do the dishes, but she wasn't about to walk out on the catwalk to the spring or even go outside to light the stove and heat water. She did what she could, wrapping the cornbread in tin foil and covering what was left of the salad and the potatoes and setting them in the cupboard, although she feared they would turn black. She found that the bucket of water she'd gotten earlier was still half full, and she set the dishes and silverware in the dishpan, poured the water over them, and left them to soak. But then, frightened because she had nothing else to do and frightened, too, by her soft footfalls, which she had commended to the darkness and silence pressing around the tree house, she climbed up on her cot and sat on her feet with her back against the wall. She felt a little too vulnerable to lie down.

After she'd been huddled against the wall for no more than ten minutes—although it seemed like a lot longer—she realized that this new, rich, free person she had become desperately needed to pee. To slide down the rope and go to the outhouse was unthinkable. She wouldn't even be able to climb back up again. To hang her buns over the edge of the catwalk and piss into a black and threatening void where Billy Wayne Roland might be skulking and grinning made her shiver and caused the hair to rise on the back of her neck. Using the trap door wasn't much better. She wanted, by God, to know what she was mooning. Sally Ann Shaw, whether the old or the new, had guts, but she wasn't up to mooning the possible agent of her own death and destruction. Ironically, the thought made her discomfort all the greater, made her kidneys burn and the pressure in her bladder seem unbearable, but she determined to bear it, either until Toots returned or the sun rose, whichever came first.

# 9

But a little less than an hour later she got down off the cot; peed in one of Toots' enameled cooking pots; crept to the door; flung pot, pee, and all into the pitch-black, woodsy night; and was back on her cot almost before the faint tintinnabulation proved the dark wasn't bottomless. "Take that," she muttered to whatever might be slinking about down below with piss in its hair.

Giddy with relief she hugged her knees to her chest and prepared to wait out the night. But sometime later when Toots called out below the tree house, the sound got into her dreams.

She was standing before the small stucco house on the edge of town where she'd been raised, watching the man across the road call his cow. "Hey. Hey. Whooee," he called, and the gentle brindle animal with its huge, mild eyes and black face ambled, full-uddered and somehow out of rhythm with itself, toward where the man had eased through the fence with feed bucket, milk bucket, and stool. She seemed to herself to be a child, barefooted, red-kneed, and wearing a chemise, but at the same time, fully grown and deep in philosophical conjecture about why she hadn't become, and would not become, a great singer. The problem, as she saw it, was irreversible. She hadn't been poor enough. She'd never been hungry, or without shoes, or spent a winter shivering in a house with cracks in the walls and cardboard set in empty window frames. She held her father to blame for the steady, mediocre wage he made on the county road crew. He provided food and heat and clothes, all marginal but adequate, and never had a serious illness or accident, went to church nearly every Sunday, and only occasionally took his pay and went on a toot. Had he been chronically unemployed, a drunkard, or partially paralyzed, she would have been able to buy him a mansion by now with miles of painted white fence around his green meadows and prize Tennessee walking horses, which, with bewildered pride, he could watch from his veranda while he tried to get accustomed to drinking his whiskey from a glass rather than from a bottle hidden in a paper bag. And her mother could have worn jewels, had her hair tinted, her nails done, and all the rooms of her mansion cleaned for her, if only she had washed clothes on a washboard or walked barefooted through the snow to scrub floors so she could buy medicine for her babies; but no, she'd had to be a sweet, ineffectual woman whose suffering came in ordinary doses and who merely went about with a slightly dazed, somewhat fearful look in her eyes as though any minute someone would ask her a question she couldn't, for the life of her, answer. Sally Ann stood underneath the mimosa tree in full neon bloom in front of her small stucco house and knew she'd been cheated of the pain necessary to lend her voice the hard, sweet edge it needed and instruct the ballads she might have written. Oh, but that was her trouble all right, or most of it —the rest was knowing what her trouble was. "Well damn it to hell," she told herself while the man across the road called, "Whooee! Hey! Hey! Whoee!" and the cow came on as full of motion as a go-go dancer, her udders moving one way, her hips another, and her brisket yet another. "Whhoooee!"

When her eyes popped open, she knew at once who was calling, and she scrambled off the cot and flung the trapdoor back. She could just make out Toots standing below, his face raised to her at the center of its flowing beard and hair like a great, damaged flower. "The rope," he said, and she dropped the complicated strands of rope through the hole. Toots put one foot in a loop and began to hoist himself slowly upward while the pulley over her head squeaked and

Toots rotated first one way and then the other until he raised himself at last into the soft yellow lamplight and pawed with his free foot at the edge of the trap door. "Give me a push," he told her, but she caught him by the top of his pants and belt and drew him to her, bracing her feet and arching her back until he could step down against her.

Somehow her dream had damaged her sense of being new, as though in her dreams, at least, she was all ages at once, both girl and woman, a creature for whom nothing could be renounced or completely forgotten. But she was so happy not to be keeping secrets and so happy not to be alone, she hugged him anyway.

"I walked all the way into town and then all the way back to the interstate, but it wasn't there," Toots said, trying to adjust to her arms around him and her head against his chest. It was an adjustment he could only make—after a few palsied, hesitant motions—by holding her as well. "Somebody else could have stolen it again," he told her. "Or the police could have picked it up, but hell," he said, "nobody's gonna find you here. If he'd got the police after you, maybe . . ." he said, but she'd already told him that Billy Wayne Roland couldn't, wouldn't dare, try to sic the police, not when he'd raped her, not when she could tell them he dealt in cocaine and all sorts of other drugs; ". . . maybe then somebody might track you down, but Mr. Roland's not going to find you. He couldn't know there's even a place back here for you to be," he said, but she held him with a kind of earnestness that seemed anything but convinced.

"I was afraid to move while you were gone," she said, her breath a series of soft explosions against his breastbone. "I felt like he was around somewhere."

"Nobody's around here," he said. "Anyway, after what you did to him, I doubt he'd be able to bother you if you called him on the phone and gave him directions."

"He has people who work for him, and they do anything he tells them to."

"They won't find you either," he said, but the soft, steady

beating of her heart made him unsure as if, somehow, her apprehensions were being softly hammered into him. "I wouldn't go walking around in public though, I guess."

"No," she said, "I won't," and she stirred slightly as if to move away, which made him feel oddly culpable. He released her instantly only to find that he no longer knew what to do with his arms and hands. Did they always hang down like that? What in hell did he do with them ordinarily, he wondered.

But Sally Ann was gazing about the room and nodding her head as though she didn't notice him at all. Then she looked down at her fancy dress and gave a little snort of laughter. She raised her arms as though she might pirouette and pose to show it off to its best effect, but she merely let her arms drop to her sides again. "What a joke," she said. "For the first time in my life I'm rich, and I can't even go buy a card of bobby pins." Suddenly she began to laugh. "Jesus Christ," she said, "I need some jeans and sneakers and shorts and underwear and blouses and a goddamned toothbrush and a hairbrush and some deodorant and . . ."

Toots waved an arm vaguely as though to dismiss such matters. "I can go into town and get anything you need," he said. "I can do it tomorrow."

She took him in, head to foot, at a single glance; and, although she did not wish to be rude or ungrateful, the flesh-colored Band-Aid sealing one eye, his none too clean khaki trousers, his purple T-shirt—no doubt it had once been navy blue—and his high-top black basketball shoes didn't exactly recommend his taste.

"Make a list," he told her.

She laughed until her eyes grew wet, and then it wasn't funny anymore. She sat down at the table and tried to compose herself.

"I should have thought, myself, that you needed things," he said. He was a little embarrassed and not at all sure why she was laughing, but he put it down to the strain she'd been under. No doubt some minor and momentary fit. As for himself, he didn't even own a toothbrush. Every day he wet the tip of his forefinger against his tongue, dipped into a box of baking soda, and then scrubbed his teeth and gums vigorously, dipping his finger into the box of soda now and again for more. A finger made a good enough toothbrush for him. Every third day he used salt rather than soda. It worked fine. His gums stayed healthy and his teeth white. Deodorant made his armpits itch, always had, and since the day he'd driven the Buick to the bluff, he'd given up the silly stuff. It was his notion that nervousness made him stink, and he'd left that sort of thing behind along with suits, ambition, and polite social lies. He bathed fairly often, at least during the warm months, and he thought he smelled just fine. Although he supposed it was a matter of conjecture how someone else might think he smelled. But in any case, he hadn't given her needs a thought. He considered her where she sat at the table, wiping her eyes, shaking her head, and still having feeble little fits of giggling; and he said, "Tomorrow morning I'll go into town as soon as the stores open and get what you want if you don't think you'll be afraid by yourself."

"No," she said, "it's just being here at night that scares me. I won't mind being by myself in the daylight."

"I'll rig a pulley for the ladder before I leave," he said. "But I guess I can go on and put it down now in case you need . . . if you want . . . I mean for the outhouse," he said.

"Don't put it down. I'm just fine," she said. "I'd feel better if the ladder stayed up at night, and anytime you're not around. Maybe when it's broad daylight and I can check out everything on this side of the river, I can let it down long enough to pee." For a moment she seemed to study the darkness pressing up against the windows. "But I don't know," she said and shook her head gravely. "You might find a chamber pot on that list tomorrow."

"Well," he said, wondering if she was being funny or serious, wondering if they still made or sold such an item.

She gave him a wan smile and kept her eyes on his face

so long that it should have made him uncomfortable, but it did not. The scrutiny she gave him was fond and warm. "You know," she said, "you may be the nicest man I ever met in all my life."

Somehow the remark made him feel instantly sad and old. Still, he saw no percentage in denying it; that would likely only make her insist. "Well," he said, "if Billy Wayne Roland is a fair sample, I guess I ought to have the title."

"Ha," she said and light danced in her eyes, "that son of a bitch doesn't even appear on my list." And swift as a child, she was up from the table, had caught his bearded face between her hands and kissed him. Her lips, soft, warm, and sweet, were against his and gone so quickly, they might not have been there at all. "God, but I'm tired all of a sudden," she said. "I feel like I could sleep for a week."

"Do you need anything?" he asked.

She shook her head.

"All right then," he said and took one of the lanterns, but he paused just before the rough curtain that separated the tree house from the cave. He wanted to tell her something, but whatever it was refused to come to mind, and what had been a significant pause became awkward while she waited, and he did too, for what he might say. He cleared his throat and still found no words to suit his feelings. "Well, I'll bid you good night then," he told her at last.

"Good night," she said.

And he entered the shallow cave where he paused again, as though what he had meant to say to her might come to him yet, but it didn't come. Suddenly feeling weary and worn himself, he set his lantern down beside the narrow bunk he'd made from a plywood door that had washed down the river to him years before. With a hammer and chisel he'd worked on a natural stone shelf until it would accept one edge of the door and had set two rough driftwood legs under the other. The mattress was made of a piece of foam rubber he'd bought and wrapped in a cotton blanket. It was a comfortable place to sleep, and he took off his shoes, blew out the lantern, and lay down upon it. The darkness of the cave pressed around him although the lantern in the other room made the curtain, itself an army surplus blanket, turn dull gold and flicker, now and again, with her shadow passing to and fro. He lay with his arms folded behind his head, and, at last, it came to him what he had wanted to say. He had wanted to explain that his convictions were being overthrown and his arguments undone, not by a greater logic, but by unfair and preemptory emotion. But he couldn't have explained such a thing because he couldn't quite think it into words; he could only feel it working on him. He would have said something silly and senseless if he'd said anything at all. He would have told her he'd spent years and years alone with no sense of being lonely and feared he was going to lose the knack.

# 10

Billy Wayne Roland watched the nurse for even a hint of smugness, but she was crisp and efficient, shaking down the thermometer with expert little snaps, raising the tent of her eyebrows just enough to let him know he was to open his mouth, placing two cool fingers on his wrist and watching the second hand of her watch as it measured his general good health. No, she was absolutely matter-of-fact even when she tossed back the sheet to check his mangled cock and adjust the catheter tube so he had a little more slack before she clipped the tube again to the sheet at the edge of the bed. It would have driven him mad if even one nurse had winked to another at his expense, or had to stifle laughter, or tried to make a joke. But they either didn't know what had happened to him, or they were very professional.

Only one had showed any emotion at all, and that was a very young one who had come in, already rosy-faced, to give him a sponge bath and had gotten frightened when he'd had one of his treacherous, arbitrary hard-ons. He'd sucked his breath in through his clenched teeth and howled curses. Every damned stitch felt like it was ripping out. "I'll get someone," she told him and, glowing red, rushed into the hall never to return. But a moment later a granite-faced nurse, about sixty, came through the door; snatched a washrag out of his little alcove bathroom; dumped ice water on it from the sweating stainless steel pitcher beside his bed; and without so much as a beg your pardon, slapped it around his dick. He wasn't sure whether the shock or the relief was greater, but his erection withered away, and he'd kept a washrag and the ice water handy ever since. No, he couldn't claim they'd made fun of him, although he watched for the least sign of it, which kept him tense.

Jerry, though, who lounged against the windowsill in his nubby off-white jacket and his cute little loafers with no socks, and his T-shirt with a collar like the top of somebody's long johns—God, but he looked like some rich little college wimp—Jerry had a smug expression on his face. And Esco was grinning like an idiot, but Esco grinned all the time, no matter what.

Billy Wayne kept his angry glance on the two of them while the nurse fluffed his pillow, raised the head of his bed, and shoved a little paper cup at him with two pills and one capsule in it—one of the damned things was supposed to keep him from getting hard-ons, but he didn't know which one, and anyway it didn't always work.

"Time to take our medicine," the nurse said and plucked the thermometer from his lips. She read it at a glance and returned it to her metal cart while he emptied the paper cup in his mouth. She held a glass of water in front of his face. "Drink it all, Mr. Roland," she said. "We need lots and lots of water."

When she had pushed her metal cart out of his room and turned down the tiled hall, Jerry wanted to say, "And how's our sore dick today?" but he didn't have the courage. "When do they say you can get out of here?" he asked instead.

"Friday," Billy Wayne said, "if the swelling goes down."

Jerry tried to think of something serious to keep from laughing, remembered the forty-five dollars he'd handed over to get the Lincoln, and didn't feel like laughing anymore. "Your car's in the lot, almost under your window," he said. "Cost me forty-five dollars to pick it up." He gave his head a little sideways cock. "We're running into a few expenses," he said. Ordinarily Billy Wayne might have taken a hundred-dollar bill from his silver money clip and slapped the bill into the breast pocket of Jerry's T-shirt or coat; Billy Wayne liked such bigshot gestures, but this time he merely lay in the hospital bed without moving a muscle, looking pasty-faced and grim.

"Keep a goddamned tab," he said. "Is the car all right?"

"Not a scratch," Jerry said. "She left it beside the road with the keys in the ignition. Just didn't have any gas in it."

A nurse passed by in the hall, and right after her, a middle-aged couple hesitated, looked in, and went on, the woman with a robe folded over her arm, the man carrying a vase of flowers. Billy Wayne motioned for Esco to close the door, and then in a softer voice said, "Did you find out where that bitch went?"

Jerry cocked his head again in the wise-assed manner that reminded Billy Wayne how little he liked him. He would, he decided, find a way to get rid of Jerry once he got things under control, but in the meantime Jerry was clever and absolutely without scruples. And if Sally Ann could be found, Jerry was the only man he had who was capable of clearing that matter up for good and with no fuss. He didn't trust Jerry's loyalty, but he had faith in his cold efficiency. Esco, on the other hand, was loyal and would do anything he was told, but you had to stand over him and watch him every minute because he had no brains. Jesus, Billy Wayne thought, who would have guessed some little stray no-talent bitch could cause so much trouble. He'd had to come up with another quarter of a million to make his buy, which was sixty-five thousand more than he could lay his hands on. He'd given his lawyer power of attorney and got him to raise it through legitimate sources. But he didn't like it. He didn't like to make bank mortgages unless the money was needed for the club or the music store. He didn't like to leave paper trails that couldn't be easily explained. But it was the best he could do from a goddamned hospital bed. That rotten bitch, he thought, listening, with bile rising in his throat, to Jerry tell about checking the bus station and the taxi stand. He had half a dozen reasons to want to settle her account, when any one, by itself, would have been enough. "What?" he said.

"I don't have any doubt of it," Jerry was saying; "she left the car and ran into the woods. We followed her all the way to the bank of a river."

Billy Wayne shook his head and frowned in confusion. "What river?" he said. "What would she do that for?" He grimaced suddenly as one of the sharp, rending pains that afflicted his penis from time to time ran its course and passed. "Christ!" he said, "say something that makes sense!"

"I'm just telling you what we found," Jerry said.

"Did she wade across? What? What?" Billy Wayne asked, color rising to his cheeks, his eyes looking bilious and crazed.

"It's a big ole river," Esco said, "and deep. I waded in, didn't I, Jerry?"

Billy Wayne looked from one of them to the other. "That cunt must have fixed it up to meet somebody!"

Jerry shook his head. "The car was out of gas," he said. "The only thing that makes any sense is that she drove it until it stopped and then got out like an idiot and ran." He loved to catch Billy Wayne being dumb. It made him feel that some day he'd have twice the money and power Billy Wayne had. It only stood to reason. He shrugged and said, "She might have drowned, maybe even on purpose. She might have gone off somewhere, gotten back to the road some way we didn't notice, but I think she might still be around there somewhere. It's just a feeling," he said. He shrugged and arched an eyebrow while Billy Wayne glared at him.

"If she left the engine running, sooner or later it would run out of gas," Billy Wayne said.

He hadn't thought of that, and it humbled him. He could feel a slight flush mounting to his eyes. "That would be a dumb thing to do," he said.

"Dumber than what you claim she did?" Billy Wayne asked.

He could feel his temples tingle with humiliation, although he felt Billy Wayne's point was a poor one, since, somehow, it *would* be dumber to have made plans, to have thought things out, and then to have parked the car so conspicuously and left such an obvious trail; that would be to argue sense and nonsense at the same time. But he knew he'd lost the verbal battle to a quicker tongue and to the power of position. If he'd been the boss, he'd have destroyed Billy Wayne's argument at once.

With a little jerk of his head Billy Wayne motioned to Esco. "Go downstairs and get me a pack of cigarettes," he told him, "and shut the door behind you." When Esco had ambled ponderously into the hallway and closed the door again, Billy Wayne said, "Look, I want you to find her, get that briefcase back, and then I want you to slit her silly, fuckin throat. If she was crazy enough to do what she did, then she's crazy enough to do anything; and I don't want anyone to lay eyes on her again, alive or dead. I want her burned to ashes, sunk to the bottom of the river, ground into bone meal and fed to somebody's hogs; hell, it's up to you, but I don't want anything left of her to turn up later. You're the only one I've got who can get it done right. I'll make it worth your while. Take Esco with you. Dumb as he is, he can come in handy. I'll even give him a little bonus, a couple of thousand or so to keep him happy. But you're the one to get it done." A sharp, searching pain cored his penis and seemed to reach even into his bowels. "Goddamn!" he said and gritted his teeth.

Jerry would have preferred to have a figure quoted, but he didn't quite have the nerve to push. He raised his hands in a gesture meant to show, if not helplessness, at least a broad range of possibilities. "She could be dead already," he said. "Or anywhere from Maine to Mexico. I've just got this feeling."

"Look, prove to me she's dead and I'll make it worth your time," Billy Wane said. "But you get that briefcase back and grind that bitch into chicken feed, and you won't have to worry about anything for a long, long time."

Each looked the other in the eye and saw what he wanted

to see, but each had a hard little fist of deceit in his heart.

"Keep all this quiet. All of it," Billy Wayne said. "I know the wops have been smelling around my operation. I know they have. They always smell money when it's there. And weakness too, goddamn it. We've got to look tight as a bluebird's cunt. We've got to look like a closed shop."

Esco came through the door then and handed Billy Wayne a pack of mentholated Trues. "All right," Billy Wayne said in a less conspiratorial voice, "Sandy's got the money for the buy ready at the music store, and here's their number." He snatched open a drawer in his bedside table, scribbled a telephone number on a note pad, and shoved it toward Jerry. "They're staying at the Maxwell House and unhappy as hell over the delay. Shit, do what you can to smooth it over, but get the stuff, and then get that other business done."

Jerry took the scrap of paper and shoved it in his coat pocket. He motioned Esco out of the room again with a nod of his head, and considered Billy Wayne a moment where he lay, spraddle-legged and ludicrous in the hospital bed. "Don't worry about a thing," he told Billy Wayne. "Just lie back and take it easy." It was a small piece of sarcasm he couldn't seem to deny himself, but he waited until he got into the hall before he grinned.

Billy Wayne seized the side of his bed and went rigid with another of those terrible pains that started in his cock and could wind up almost anywhere. He considered buzzing for a nurse, but he didn't want one in the room with him, and anyway the pains, though fierce, never lasted more than a moment, not, anyway, unless he got an erection. The pain then was unthinkable, almost as unthinkable as imagining Sally Ann out of his reach and living the high life on his money. She had to, by God, pay. Getting his revenge was almost as important to him as seeing to it that she didn't put him or his operation in jeopardy.

He thought he knew women. He did know women, that was what was so goddamned maddening about it. He knew everything about them, and still he'd been deceived, which somehow didn't prove to him that he didn't know them, but simply that their built-in random craziness had to be taken a lot more seriously than he'd supposed; they might not merely break dishes. And what had started the fight to begin with? A matter of no great importance. He'd asked her to throw a little fuck on a very important man in the country music business, a very important producer. It wasn't going to do her career any good, but she didn't know that. The man had admired her at the club in her skimpy little cocktail waitress uniform, and Billy Wayne—generously and because it was good business—said he'd send her over to his place and see to it that she treated him right. And what the hell, maybe the fat old fucker would have done something for her. Who could tell? But no, Sally Ann Shaw couldn't do a favor, had to act like a goddamned virgin all of a sudden. It just wasn't anything to get so mad at. Sure, she might have gotten mad about her apartment being used as a cocaine drop, but he hadn't even gotten around to telling her that.

He'd tried to slap some sense into her and straighten her out, but she wouldn't have it—cursed him and hit him and kicked—God, but he hated a woman with a smart, nasty mouth. So he'd showed her a thing or two. Sure he'd been rough, but if he'd enjoyed it, then you could bet she'd enjoyed it too. He'd never known that principle to fail. It was their nature. Hell, he'd expected things to be all right afterward. He'd expected her to be docile, maybe even apologetic. God, but he'd shoved it to her and held nothing back, and thinking about what he'd done to her, how she had cried out and struggled and moaned, made him snatch up his washcloth and pitcher of ice water, but it had gotten a little ahead of him, and he ground his teeth and clamped his eyes shut until tears of pain and rage dampened his cheeks.

When he could loosen his grip on the side of the bed, he savored the revenge Jerry would take on her for him. Later, when he got well, he'd get rid of Jerry. There was a landfill dump where he'd make Esco dig Jerry's sacked-up body down into the garbage. The bulldozers would finish the burying in a few days. Then, by God, the slate would be clean.

But what if Jerry couldn't find her? He ground his teeth at the thought, but he had to admit its possibility. He'd get rid of that goddamned Jerry anyway. As for Sally Ann, he promised himself he'd take revenge on fifty women to make up for her. But he'd find her one day. He'd make a fucking hobby of looking for her and inventing new ways to settle the score. He knew why she'd gone crazy; it was suddenly clear to him: it was because he hadn't let her sing in his club —sure, he'd made the promise in an expansive moment, just the way he'd promised to send her to the promoter's place. It was his generosity that had gotten him into trouble, his style. A little petulant regret haunted the stations of his brain. He should probably have let her sing, and probably he shouldn't have promised to send her by the promoter's place, or hit her quite so hard, or hurt her quite so much. But, Jesus, she didn't have to go crazy on him. The vicious little bitch. His cock ached in a resigned, stubborn way in the aftermath of his hard-on, and his ass was in a cold, damp puddle from the ice water he'd had to use. Suddenly the regret he'd felt only a moment before became a rage so violent it shook him and caused his bed to set up a momentary, thin rattling. She'd robbed him, mangled the very instrument of his manhood, even, he suggested, meant to kill him, although she'd only managed to give him one hell of a concussion. For certain she'd made him a laughingstock and a fool, leaving him for Esco to find just before that damned Puerto Rican and that damned Texan arrived with the coke. At least Esco had gotten him out of there and to the hospital, and so saved him the humiliation of being seen by anyone except the doctors and nurses in the emergency room. He was torn between gratitude and an urge to get rid of Esco, too, for what he had witnessed. Although with Esco you couldn't be sure how much, if anything, registered. Jerry, thank God, had been working at the club.

He felt assailed. He'd come into town fifteen years ago as

the manager and agent of a crummy little band, and now he owned a fancy club and a music store that sold everything from guitar picks to organs, everything from records to stereo systems. And he had a drug business that threatened to make more money than either of the others and was, by God, tax free. He was getting big, so big that the mob would be trying to move in on him very soon. He knew it. He knew he'd have to deal with it. His customers, however, would be strong allies. It wasn't that they cared so much about the law. They were often suspicious and resentful of the law in any case since it was so often imposed on them from somewhere else: the county seat, the state or federal government. It was as if they felt laws were some kind of Yankee plot to keep them from making moonshine, or keeping the niggers in line, or otherwise doing what they wanted and needed to do. There was a strange independence, a strange, very local patriotism that made them want to do business with another good ole boy and not some damned foreign crook. No, they wouldn't like giving their business to the Mafia, by God. That prejudice and patriotism was a part of them, he felt sure, just as in the deepest chamber of his brain, it was part of him too. He wanted to nationalize crime, goddamn it, just the way an Arab country would nationalize its oil fields. He could start a secret campaign. Don't sell America out, support your local criminal. Native outlaws were a great resource, he decided. It gave him a warm, secure feeling to imagine all illegal operations run by real Americans. Such a situation seemed somehow properly governable and healthy. He liked to imagine himself as the head man all across the country, the big boss who could dispense punishment or rewards at his whim. If he was clever and absolutely without mercy, perhaps it might be possible. Perhaps snuffing Sally Ann Shaw and Jerry Tetler would be a good beginning—show them all he wasn't someone to fool with.

He lay basking in the warmth of that vision, his cock aching in a dull, far-off sort of way, until more practical considerations edged the daydream out of his thoughts.

Both Esco and Jerry were familiar with where and how everyone liked their cocaine or uppers or downers delivered. One female singer had to snort two lines exactly half an hour before she performed, and she wanted it delivered to her dressing room in a box of a dozen red roses. Someone else would want it to come in a guitar case, another in a pair of boots, and all of the big stars used intermediaries to pick it up from Esco or Jerry. He'd have to call Sandy at the music store and tell him as much as he could. Sandy always took the orders and kept things straight, but he'd never made deliveries.

He didn't like mucking up the works and changing things around; he didn't like making his customers nervous. He wanted everything to run like a well-oiled machine. He didn't want anyone, particularly any outside interest, to see the slightest weakness or flaw in his operation. He picked up the phone and dialed the music store, annoyance rising in his throat like bile. He was going to get an ulcer; he knew it.

Toots didn't attract much attention at Hobb's Riverside Market or down at the Army-Navy store, where, maybe once every six months, he went to buy some socks or britches or a new pair of basketball shoes; but he hadn't much more than entered the hushed, air-conditioned chill of the department store when he realized most of the salesgirls and the few early morning shoppers were watching him as though he were some sort of crazy derelict . . . wino . . . bum . . . only God knew what. He hadn't considered the figure he might cut in such a place and he was immediately and deeply embarrassed. He should have tied his hair back in a ponytail, worn his eye patch, and put on his going-to-Nashville clothes. But he'd no more than had the idea when he knew it wouldn't have helped either: all sorts of strange people rode the buses these days, and, in Nashville, he was generally taken for just another eccentric entertainer. Dozens of times strangers had insisted he was someone named Doctor Hook, and often he was unable to convince them otherwise. Once he'd even given an autograph in order to be left in peace; a very heavy woman in a maternity dress simply would not turn loose of his coatsleeve until he did. But he could see that no one in the department store had mistaken him for a celebrity. They were all watchful and nervous as deer. Be calm and go about your business, he told himself, but it had been so long since he'd had any business in such a place, he wasn't sure just how to act. Anyway, commerce of any sort had always made him strangely shy and uncomfortable, and it was with something close to panic that he saw one of the salesgirls square her shoulders and approach him, trying to manage a professional smile that flickered on and off uncertainly like a defective light.

"Can I help you with something?" she asked, as though she very much doubted that she could, as though, in fact, she was pretty certain he was in the wrong store if not altogether in the wrong part of town.

Flustered, his vision blurred by embarrassment, Toots consulted the scrap of paper bag on which Sally Ann had drawn up her list and saw, with horror, the first item: six pairs of nylon bikini panties, size five. He couldn't speak, and a moment later, he couldn't even seem to understand the notation. Did that mean twelve panties? Pairs of socks he could understand. Pairs of shoes made perfect sense. But pairs of panties? Maybe they called them that because they had two legholes; but a shirt had two armholes, and you'd be a nut to ask for a pair of shirts unless you meant to buy two. The subtleties of the language were suddenly beyond him, but it was clear enough that, no matter how he said it, if he asked for panties, the woman was sure to take him for some kind of pervert. A fetishist. A kidnapper. A sex maniac. A transvestite. She'd fall back in horror. She'd call the police. He stared at the list, unable to move or speak, and noticed dirt under his fingernails. How could it be there? Early that morning while the mist was still rising from the river he'd squatted on the stern of the johnboat like an aborigine to scrub himself all over with a cake of soap—hair, beard, and all—before he flopped into the smoking water to rinse. The dirt under his fingernails, alone, seemed a crime; and the scrap of brown paper covered in a penciled, childish scrawl was grotesquely vulgar.

"Sir?" the salesgirl said.

He swallowed and felt his Adam's apple bobble. He'd promised, after all, to return with everything on the list. "Pants," he blurted suddenly. "I have to have some pants."

"Oh," the salesgirl said, obviously much relieved, "then you'll want the men's department. It's just over there," she said and arched her arm and finger to indicate the left rear of the store some thirty yards away. "They'll help you."

"Yes," he said, "yes," and immediately took himself off in the direction she'd pointed out. And oddly enough, he'd gotten only a few aisles away when the confusion seemed to lift from his mind just as quickly as it had descended. Of course, he thought, a pair of trousers, a pair of shorts, a pair of pliers; the language was full of pairs of things; it was merely an expression, nothing to get hysterical about.

The clerk in the men's department seemed almost as unsure of him as the salesgirl had, but Toots was vastly relieved. However undomesticated or odd he might look, he wasn't likely to be taken for some kind of sexual degenerate.

He bought a pair—*of course, a pair*—of seersucker trousers with elastic around the backside of the waist, putter pants, the clerk called them; he bought a knit shirt; and he bought a pair of rope-soled canvas shoes. The shirt and shoes were beige, the pants, a modest blue and white. He put them on in the dressing room and came out before a three-way mirror to inspect himself. He looked neater, but something terribly fundamental remained unchanged. He could do nothing about the divot of bone missing from the bridge of his nose and his temple, or about his missing eye. But the beard and hair . . . ? Hmmm, he thought, there wasn't a great deal of advantage in looking like a well-dressed deviate. "I'll take them," he told the clerk and went back in the dressing room to collect his basketball shoes and his clothes, which looked to him suddenly—as perfectly familiar as they were—more like cleaning rags than actual clothes.

Idly he watched the clerk scribble on the sales slip. Sally Ann had given him three hundred dollars, and he had taken as much or more from one of the coffee cans he kept as containers on the top shelf above his sideboard. For years he'd cashed his disability checks and poked the money absentmindedly, disinterestedly into the cans. He kept nails and screws in some of the cans too, and was often disappointed, when he needed a nail, to find himself looking into a can stuffed with money. It cost him very little to live, and the fish he sold to Hobb's Market more often than not took care of his needs. He'd meant to buy what Sally Ann wanted from the coffee can money in case she might change her mind and decide to send that Nashville bastard's fortune back.

When the clerk had added up the bill, he pushed it doubtfully across the counter. "Seventy-eight fifty," he said in a voice that seemed both to convey sympathy and expect rebuke; but when Toots reached into the pocket of the stained, threadbare pants he carried and fetched out a great handful of bills, the clerk's head snapped back as if he'd been struck. Toots counted out the money and shoved the rest into the new trousers he wore, and then remembering, retrieved Sally Ann's crisp bills from another pocket of the old pants and tucked them away neatly in the pocket of his new knit shirt. The clerk cleared his throat. "Uh," he said, "would you like to see anything else . . . a nice summer sportcoat maybe, or a suit perhaps?"

Toots thought it over. "A bag," he said.

"Pardon?" the clerk said.

"A sack or something to put my old clothes in."

"Surely, of course," the clerk said and, from under the counter, produced a plastic bag with handles built into the top. "How about socks? Underwear? Ties?"

Outside again, while he walked the streets and looked for a barber pole, the light and heat seemed dazzling and oppressive even though it was not yet ten o'clock. He felt peculiar, light-headed, even a little queasy in the stomach. His new clothes didn't seem to suit his shape like his old ones and had, besides, a faint spicy odor a bit like a new car. Maybe that was his trouble, he thought. Or maybe it was the sudden shock of coming out of the air-conditioning or out of his profoundly ridiculous embarrassment. But on some level or other he knew it was something else. He knew he wasn't going to so much trouble merely to make it easier to buy the things on Sally Ann's list. He wouldn't let himself think about it deeply, but he understood his motivation wasn't so simple as all that, and he suspected it was working violence on his spirit.

The legend on the window said *A Cut Above,* and he walked past the place twice, looking it over, before he decided to go in. It didn't look like a barber shop exactly, but there were men inside getting haircuts. What the hell, he thought, and stepped across the threshold; he wasn't quite himself anyway and hardly knew what he might do next. "Can I get a shave in here?" he asked. "And a haircut."

"Do you have an appointment?" the barber at the first chair asked with a stagey flourish of scissors and comb over his customer's head.

Toots admitted that he did not, but it turned out not to matter. A female barber a few stations down had just had a late cancellation and agreed to take him.

He was surprised that no one paid any particular attention to him in this place. The woman who seated him at last in her chair even tried to change his mind about his beard. "Are you sure you wouldn't prefer a trim?" she asked him. "I could give it a nice shape."

"I want a clean shave," he said.

She cupped the sides of his beard in her palms and cocked her head first one way and then the other with her lower lip stuck out in a pout. "Awwwwhh," she said, but she took up her scissors and set to work.

He looked in the mirror while great tufts and nests of beard fell around him. Fascinated, he watched the line of his jaw appear, his chin, the hollows of his cheeks. "Even the mustache?" she asked him, and when he nodded, she said, "Awwwhh," again and stuck out her lip, but she snipped away until, in blurred, stubbed outline, a face he hadn't seen in nearly ten years and didn't altogether recognize began to look at him out of the mirror. Oh, there was a family resemblance, he supposed, but the fellow looking back at him was a little hollower in the cheek and longer in the lip than he would have supposed, and the wild mane of hair fanning out, which was no longer met and somehow subdued by the beard, looked a little clownish, as if, say, he'd just stuck his finger in a light socket. But in the next moment his barber wrapped the strange face away in a steaming hot towel, and he closed his eye, wondering what was becoming of him. "You've got just beautiful hair," she told him. "Blond and red and white. Beautiful. Beautiful. Would you like to see some styles?"

"No," he said from beneath his towel, "just cut it." Somehow, already not quite recognizing his own face, he had no firm vision of how he wished to look. He would take what he got. "Suit yourself," he added, feeling he had already disappointed her in the matter of the beard. He merely hoped he would look better, more acceptable, younger. He and Sally Ann could get used to his new face together, since, however it turned out, it would surely be less outrageous than his old one.

The woman's hands were in his hair, brushing it, fussing with it, but he kept his eye closed even when she tilted his chair back, removed the hot towel, lathered his face, and began to shave him. She had a sharp razor and a gentle touch, and it was pleasant to have her pull the skin tight along his jawbone, or along his neck, or on his upper lip; he let her do it all and mugged no faces for her. And it was pleasant, too, when she tested her work by brushing her soft fingers against the grain of his beard. Even when she washed his face and massaged it with an aftershave, and set the chair up straight again, he didn't look at himself.

For some reason he had begun to think about his prosthetic eye. No doubt he'd needed a little reconstructive work around the socket, since the eye had fallen out once or twice in the months he'd worn it. But the last time he'd lost it, it had fallen into the river. He'd been wrestling a big channel cat aboard his boat—a fish that weighed seventy-eight pounds as it turned out—when the channel cat had somehow jarred him just right while he was leaning over the water trying to haul it in, and the eye fell, plop, into the river where it darted and shimmered down through the depths like a minnow. For almost a month after, he'd left the socket uncovered—an empty nest, a small crooked smile which he cocked at the world. But it brought him news. It was aware of the direction of the most minuscule breeze, seemed to fathom the source of sounds better than his ears, could sense the smallest changes in temperature and barometric pressure. So sensitive and keen was it that, from time to time, he would close the good eye and be surprised and disappointed when he could not see, although he knew it had been ridiculous to have supposed otherwise. But God, how the empty socket collected grit, the husks of buds, weed seeds, gnats, and, in its great sensitivity, grew inflamed. Finally, he'd had to tape it shut with a Band-Aid. Somehow that open wound seemed to him a grave metaphor, but he couldn't quite decipher its meaning.

He didn't know whether he'd slept or merely dropped into some deep reverie, but the next thing he knew, he was being vacuumed and asked how he liked what she had done. He looked into the mirror at last, and a new man looked back at him, beautifully groomed and fresh-faced, if not so young as he had hoped. "Thank you," he said. "Thank you very much." He rose and stepped across great clumps and mounds of beard and hair that circled his chair like a ring of small, furry animals shot from a tree. "Look at it all," he said in awe. "You could stuff half a sofa with it."

Having paid his bill and got out on the street again, he couldn't pass a store window without being aware of his reflection keeping pace. It matched him step for step, mannerism for mannerism. He never caught it making a single false move, and so, after a while, it ceased to surprise him quite so much; but, giddy as he was, he never quite lost a faint, odd sense of betrayal, too—an empty, sinking sensation in his stomach as though some part of him knew he was making a fundamental and irredeemable mistake.

In Woolworth's he bought a pair of dark sunglasses, and after bending the ear pieces this way and that, he managed to make the glasses fit fairly well, although the little yoke that was supposed to sit on the bridge of his nose was suspended in air. And he bought a small note pad, which carried a mechanical pencil cleverly in its binding. When he had transcribed Sally Ann's list from the torn piece of brown paper bag to the neat little note pad, he threw the original away.

He might have gone back to the first department store with little chance of being recognized, but he didn't. He found an even nicer one, and when a salesgirl asked, as cordially as if they were old friends, if she could help him, he said, "Let me see now," and flipped open the cover of his little note pad with his finger. "I'll want two pair of jeans and four pair of shorts in size seven. Six cotton T-shirts in a medium. Six pairs of bikini panties, size five, and one pair of sneakers in size six and a half." Without turning a hair and with great good cheer, the salesgirl set about showing him what he'd asked for and was very helpful with her opinions and advice. He got into the spirit of things so completely that he added a few items of his own, including a wraparound skirt, two blouses, a sun dress, and a pair of sandals. He had to call a taxi to transport all his packages to a drugstore, where he had the taxi wait while he bought a toothbrush, toothpaste, deodorant, baby lotion, mascara, hair coloring, foundation, blush, and all sorts of other things he read carefully from his list, somehow surprised each time the articles were placed on the counter before him, as though such strange products in colors like rose frost and plum radiance were absolutely ordinary and everyday.

It was after two o'clock in the afternoon and smotheringly hot when the taxi dropped him on the begrimed and littered semicircle of earth in front of Hobb's Riverside Market, and he began to set his various packages on the hood of the taxi until he could pay the fare and find some way to carry them all without putting anything on the ground, which was a sticky compound of old crankcase oil, filth, and bottle caps. The little driver made no effort to help. He merely sat sullenly, impatiently, behind the wheel, a damp cigarette stuck in the corner of his mouth, and his nearly fleshless arm—all bone and vein and blue tattoo—cocked out the open window. When Toots paid him, tipped him two dollars, and took a precarious grip on the last of the packages, the grim little driver backed away and swung around at once as though he feared Toots might set his burdens back on the hood again to seek a better purchase. But as though he were performing some sort of dangerous balancing act, Toots carefully skirted one end of the market and went off down the uneven, worn path toward the river. He could not see exactly where he was putting his feet down, and now and again he hesitated a moment to paw tentatively at the ground in front of him until he could remember or figure out its topography. He'd seen Hobb inside the small, flyblown, plate-glass window, watching him curiously as he negotiated the parking area with his load of packages; and, before he was twenty yards down the path to the river, he heard the spring on the rear door of the market grind and strum open and then the door slap shut again, and he figured Hobb had come out to watch him struggle on toward the river. All at once he realized Hobb hadn't recognized him, never mind that he had stopped by that very morning to deliver almost a hundred pounds of catfish—having netted them from his holding pool since he hadn't been running his lines the way he should—and naturally even Hobb would be curious. No one ever arrived at his market by taxi, although once in a while someone too drunk to do otherwise might leave that way. Toots pawed at the uneven ground ahead of him and went carefully on, giggling softly to himself. No doubt Hobb would watch him until he disappeared into the willows on the riverbank, fingering his doughy forehead beneath his paper hat, unable to make any sense whatever of such a well-dressed stranger arriving by taxi only to struggle off toward the river under a mountain of department store parcels. Chiefly because he was supremely uninterested in anything beyond the workings of his little beer joint and market, Hobb never stuck his nose in anyone's business. He was a dull, quiet man with no more personality than a can of corn, but Toots suspected he might shake his head and puzzle over this matter once or twice, at least until Toots came downriver again and Hobb could see who he was. Then, abruptly, and probably without asking a single question, he'd simply forget it.

With the first glimpse he caught of his boat, he knew he was in trouble. He'd never quite realized what a scow it was. He found a grassy spot on the bank, unburdened himself, and looked unhappily at the two or three inches of dirty water that covered the scummy bottom of the johnboat; the wet gunny sacks he'd used to carry his catfish in piled in the bow; and the split-bottom chair that was the boat's only seat. It would ruin his shoes even to step into the thing, and clearly there was no way in the world to balance all his purchases on a single chair. He stood on one foot and then the other and took his shoes off. He rolled up his trousers. He took off his shirt and draped it carefully across a branch. Finally he minced fastidiously down the bank and into his boat where, with a scoop made of half a plastic Clorox bottle, he bailed very gently so as not to splash himself. He spread the gunny sacks over the inch of silt on the bottom, but he could see at once how little that was going to help, so he climbed ashore and rummaged through his old pants until he found his pocketknife and then cut small cane until he had enough to make a pallet to put the packages on. Finally, when he had everything in the boat and had hung his new shirt over the back of his chair, he pushed off and started upriver, amazed and aggravated at how much effort it took to keep from soiling himself or the things he'd bought, and how utterly impossible it was to keep from sweating. Christ, he thought, it was a full-time job just to keep clean, but he meant to try.

It took him twice as long as usual to paddle the three and a half miles home, but still his chest was slick with sweat and the waist of his trousers was damp when the johnboat rode up on the sand spit in front of the tree house. There was no sign of Sally Ann, although the ladder he'd rigged with a pulley that morning was pulled up so that its top reared above the eaves. He carried the first load of packages ashore and shouted "Hey," but there wasn't a sound from the tree house or any sign of her. He brought up the rest of the packages and then fetched his shoes and shirt. He knelt by the springhouse and washed his face, neck, and chest in the icy water and dug out his old T-shirt to use as a towel. He washed his feet, one at a time, and stuck them in his new shoes and slipped into his fancy knit shirt. "Hey," he yelled. "Hey up there, aren't you interested in all your new clothes?" He thought he saw a dim movement through one of the small windows, but the inside of the tree house was shadowy and his angle of vision was so poor he wasn't certain that he hadn't seen merely a movement of the tree-tops reflected in the window glass. "Hey," he said, "it's me. It's Toots!" and he took off the dark sunglasses and raised the damaged side of his face.

There was a furtive movement just on the other side of the screen door. "Toots?" she said tentatively.

He laughed. "Drop the ladder down," he said, "I've got all kinds of stuff down here."

Half her face appeared around the door frame, and she paused there a moment before she pushed the door partway open and peered at him narrowly. "Christ," she said, "I didn't know who in the hell you were. What did you do to yourself?"

The question seemed, all at once, too complicated and personal to answer and he felt himself blush. The night before he'd gotten hugged when he left to go look for the car and hugged again when he'd returned; somehow he'd hoped for at least as much this time. He felt he'd been caught out at something. "I just got a shave and a bit of a haircut," he said at last. "That's all." He looked down at his new shirt and pants and shoes and turned his palms up in a gesture of futility. "And I got some different clothes, I guess."

She came out on the catwalk then and loosened the rope

tied to the railing. She was wearing nothing more than a slip in the heat, and the buds of her nipples, deep, dark pink, showed through, which made it impossible, somehow, for him to look at her. The pulley squeaked and squeaked and the foot of the ladder slid down in front of him.

It took four trips up to the tree house before he had all her things inside, and she hadn't hugged him once. What was more, when she looked at him, it was a strange sort of sidelong look, almost as if they'd only just met, or as if she'd grown suddenly shy and suspicious of him. Each article of clothing she unwrapped seemed to get nearly the same oblique appraisal she kept giving him.

"Well," he said, "will they do all right?"

"Sure," she said. "Sure, everything is real nice." She turned slightly away from him to consider the things she'd laid aside on the table as she'd unwrapped them, and a bemused smile flickered across her mouth. "They're classy and expensive and kind of . . ." She tilted her head first one way and then the other as though she were looking for exactly the right word, and she laughed a little. "Well, they're sweet," she said.

He'd kept the skirt, blouses, sun dress, and sandals a little to one side, and he set them before her then, trying to figure out just what he wanted to say about them. "Here's some more," he told her, which was the best he could do.

He couldn't quite tell what she thought of them. At first she seemed amused, but then somehow she seemed to grow unsure and thoughtful, looking from a blouse to his face or turning one of the sandals over and over in her hands as though it were oddly formed or as though she couldn't quite guess its function. She stood up and held the sun dress against her, taking a pinch of its material at her shoulder and bracing it with her forearm against her waist. "It's beautiful, Toots," she said, "all of it. It really is. I guess it's not exactly what I would have got for myself maybe," she said and swallowed once or twice before she cocked her head and laughed again. "I go for just a hair more . . . more flash, I guess," she said. "A country singer, you know, might want to hit the eyes a little harder." She sat down again with the sun dress bunched in her lap. "You're a wonder," she said. "I didn't have any idea what sort of thing you'd come back with, but . . ." She held the sun dress up, looked at it, let it flop again into her lap, and began to laugh. It was a merry laugh, he decided, and he laughed too, although he wasn't exactly sure what was funny. "I just didn't expect anything so prim, so, I don't know, ladylike. And my God, look at you!" she said. "You look like a doctor, or a rich golf player. No," she said and pointed her finger at him, "I've got it; you look like some tragic German nobleman on the late show . . . and to think when I first saw you . . . but my God, you're almost handsome," she said, laughing. "Jesus, Jesus Christ!" She wiped her eyes and shook with laughter. "I think I must have kissed a frog."

And they both laughed until suddenly her eyes popped wide and she said, "Oh, I didn't mean it the way it sounded. I mean I didn't mean to say you were a frog because there you were all the time just hiding behind all that fuzz and fur, but for all I knew you could have been crazy or dangerous or something. Oh my," she said, "you must think I'm the one that's crazy, but you have to admit you don't talk much, so how's anyone supposed to know?" She took a deep breath and seemed to hold it. "That doesn't make any sense, does it?" she said.

"Yes," he said.

"I really wasn't kidding last night when I said you might be the nicest man I ever met, but in a way that was because I wasn't thinking of you as an ordinary person. I mean I didn't know you were handsome then or anywhere near as young." Jesus Christ, she thought to herself, why couldn't she shut up? But she knew the answer. She'd never once met a man who had anything going for him who didn't also have at least a touch of arrogance and wasn't finally more of a taker than a giver. And so she'd had Toots down as some kind of crazy old coot who was harmless and sweet, a nutty old hairball who lived in a tree. "You ought not to sneak up on a person like this," she told him. "Oh my," she said, feeling totally flustered and confused, "I need to rethink this whole thing. I need a bath." She put her sun dress down on the table and idly touched or rearranged the other clothes there, feeling, all the while, Toots' clear blue eye looking at her, blue as a cornflower, blue as the sky; and his hawkish face turned to her, watching her, waiting. All her fond feelings for him seemed to realign themselves in a way that brought a flush to her cheeks. "Oh my, what are we going to do now?" she said. "Do you think we ought to make love or what?"

"Yes," Toots said, "that's what I think." Strangely, he was only ninety percent astonished. Another ten percent of him, although it didn't dare insist, seemed to feel that such a turn of events was only natural and even, in some strange way, deserved, as though all those years by himself were fated to make him a proper lover and maybe even handsome, although he had never been handsome before. Being alone for such a great long time had somehow even taught him just the right way to fold Sally Ann into his arms. Oh, but solitude was a distant, wistful sort of lover, cool and serene and perfect, but with nothing like the warm, firm flesh of Sally Ann and with no capacity whatever to surprise him. "Oh God," Sally Ann said, fitting her body to his with a witchery that awed him, "now I got to rethink this whole damned thing."

# 12

Jerry popped a Tums in his mouth and tucked the rest of the roll into his shirt pocket. "Turn it around," he said, "and we'll go back up the road. Maybe we missed something." But he'd told Esco too late to turn before the bridge, and they had to drive across the river and into the business district of Clifton before Esco could turn. It was a narrow old iron bridge, almost too narrow for two lanes, and it rattled and clattered as they crossed. Distracted, Jerry looked down at the river through the iron braces and saw eight or ten needle-nosed gar hanging motionless just below the surface, the smallest of them almost two feet long, the largest, over three. They were sunning themselves in the slack water, but to Jerry they were only so many slender, dark shapes, since he didn't know what sort of fish they were or even if they were fish at all. He was out of patience and upset. They had followed the river as closely as the road would allow all the way into town from the spot Roland's car had been abandoned, and they hadn't seen a single marina or fishing tackle store where he could rent a boat or work up a conversation with some of the locals to see what he could find out. For the first two miles below the place Sally Ann had stopped, there was nothing but woods between the road and the river. And even when they got into town and the Bear Creek Pike became Riverside Drive, there was nothing to fire his imagination: a Big John's Barbecue; a used car lot with a dingy trailer bleeding rust through its rivets and a dozen very tired cars sitting out front; and a mile and a half farther, a seedy little grocery. Other than those three businesses, there were only small, unpretentious houses along the road, places that seemed to grow steadily shabbier as they approached the center of town until, just before the iron bridge, there was one last collapsing and abandoned house and then a ballfield with a scuffed and rutted diamond, a rusty wire backstop, and a few ancient floodlights rising high into the afternoon heat on creosoted poles. The whole area seemed hopelessly closed, as though any stranger asking questions would be bound to attract a great deal of attention and get very little information for his trouble.

Just across the bridge Esco pulled into a defunct service station and turned between the gutted stucco building and the crumbling cement island where the gas pumps had once stood, and they crossed the river again. "What are we looking for?" Esco asked, but Jerry didn't bother to answer.

Somehow when they'd trailed Sally Ann to the river, he'd felt smart and lucky, as though he were on a roll. It was as if he could sense her close by, smell her, feel her panic in the very print of her hand where she had fallen. But he didn't have that sense of her any longer. The trail seemed cold and full of possibilities he felt powerless to uncover. Perhaps that fool Roland was right and she'd met someone. The river could accommodate a small float plane very nicely, for example. And what would it matter if she had simply pulled the car over and left it running, if her next stop was three or four states away? No, he thought, Roland had provoked her and what she had done, she had done on the spur of the moment. But what if she'd planned to rip him off all along and the fight had merely happened? What if the fight had been incidental, what then? No, he thought, she would have picked a better spot to meet someone than the place he'd tracked her to. If she was going to fly out, Old Hickory Lake would have done just as well for a float plane, and it was only five miles away and civilized. And why a float plane? Any plane would do. Or hell, she could have met someone on any street corner in Nashville, and he could have driven her off in anything from a sports car to a pickup truck. It didn't make any sense. He was getting soft in the head trying to find logic where there was nothing but silliness and stupidity. The dumb bitch was much more likely to have drowned herself than to have made a sensible plan. How long, he wondered, did it take a body to float to the surface? It would be wise, he thought, for the two of them to keep an eye out for a bloated corpse floating in some backwater. But if she'd killed herself, the chances were damned slim they'd ever see that quarter of a million again. Jesus, he thought, what a waste. He could set himself up for the rest of his life on such a sum, and that goddamned Billy Wayne Roland had merely come up with another quarter of a million and made his buy as though nothing whatever had happened. He and Esco had handed it over to a nervous little Puerto Rican and a Texan with disgusting nests of hair growing out of his nostrils—just handed it over as though it were so much pocket change. The very idea that the world was full of high-grade morons who were rolling in money wrecked his sleep at night and soured his stomach during the day. "Whoa," he said, and Esco slammed on the brakes so hard Jerry had to brace himself against the dash to keep from being thrown into the windshield. Even Esco bounced off the steering wheel. "Back up, dummy, and take that dirt road down to the river."

"Well, you said whoa," Esco explained, choosing not to meet Jerry's disgusted, angry stare.

"You want to cause an accident?" Jerry said. "What if someone had been behind us?"

Esco didn't say anything.

"Idiot," Jerry said.

Esco backed up and turned down a narrow gravel road that had appeared to be only a driveway beside a shabby, turquoise-colored house. As they eased off the pavement toward the river, Jerry found himself exchanging glances with a little girl standing on the porch. Her chest and forearms, as well as the bright yellow shorts she wore, were stained with what looked like grape juice; a few cheap plastic toys littered a sofa behind her, which leaked cotton batting from a hole in one of its cushions; and she sucked the middle three fingers of one hand and watched him so steadily, her thumb and little finger sticking up by her eyes at such odd angles, she appeared to be giving him some sort of sign or making some crazy kind of obscene gesture. Christ, Jerry thought, but he had no business in such a low-life place as this. He needed to be surrounded with wealth and style and intelligent, sophisticated people, and he meant to be.

The road led to a power dam, which, by the looks of it, hadn't generated any electricity in years. An old Studebaker and a newer pickup were parked in a small loop of hard-packed earth and scrappy grass, and Jerry said, "Stop."

When he got out of the air-conditioned car, the heat and the heavy odor of the river oppressed him, but he went over to the steep escarpment below the dam and looked down. On the rocky shore beneath him, two fishermen tended rods propped on forked sticks. Good, he thought, terrific; at least he'd found someone he could have a little conversation with. Maybe he could find out something worthwhile. He motioned Esco to stay in the car and climbed down the steep path to the river. It was always best to leave Esco in the car, he was thinking. Before they'd left Nashville, he himself had changed into a pair of khakis and a T-shirt he'd worn to paint his apartment in, and he thought he looked perfectly ordinary, but he hadn't been able to do much with Esco, who had put on a sleazy pair of dress pants and a sport shirt, both of which would have been in poor taste anywhere—hell, maybe he'd look the part if he were renting shoes in some dive of a bowling alley or racking balls in some dingy pool hall; but anywhere else he looked not only out of place but somehow threatening as well. The asshole, Jerry thought, the idiot.

When he had climbed down to the river to join the fishermen, he squatted and spat, lounged and loitered like a native. He guffawed at commonplaces and found out all manner of things he didn't want to know. He found out how to make a great stink bait—kill a house cat and bury it in a plastic bag for at least six weeks, put the god-awful soup that resulted in mason jars, dip cotton balls in it, bait your hook with the cotton balls, chuck your line in the river, and be prepared to catch every catfish around. And, if for some reason you got tired of fishing, the stink bait made the best lure for fox traps there ever was; even a wily old gray couldn't resist rotten cat. He learned about Catawba worms —a great bait for any kind of fish—and how to freeze them so he could use them long after their season. He learned about willow grubs and how to build a screen box and sift river-bottom mud for them. Shoot the shit, he commanded himself through it all; squat and spit and shoot the shit.

There was no doubt in his mind that he would have made a fine actor. He had those two fishermen completely fooled, and in some odd way it was satisfying to be in disguise, to pass himself off as the driver of a bakery truck—just another good ole boy new in town—and to know that in the Camaro he had a little Smith and Wesson twenty-two pistol with a six-inch barrel and a silencer, and that if he chose to do so, he could do away with both of them with less noise than he made when he turned his head and spat—*bip, bip,* one shot each behind the ear. He felt all but omnipotent. Such perfect deceit was power. But lucky for them he had discretion too. To think about punching their tickets was no more than whimsy; it would serve no purpose. Besides, he had learned some useful things from them. He found out that no one around made a practice of renting boats, but that there were a couple of dozen boats up above the dam chained in a little slough, and no one would mind if he kept his there if he should happen to buy one. And the fellow to see about buying one was a hermit of a man who lived up the river and always had a boat or two for sale. Cheap, too, because he caught them every spring when the river flooded. A strange old codger he was, who made his living fishing the river and lived in a tree—they swore before God he did—in a tree house, to tell the whole truth about it, but it was twenty feet off the ground, right up there in the branches among the squirrels. And who could say? He might rent a boat, but he asked so little for them, it would likely be cheaper to buy. The only trouble was you damned near had to have a boat already to get to his place. Oh, you could catch him at Hobb's Market, just up the street, when he sold his fish or stopped in for a beer. Or you could leave word at the market for him because he came in with his fish every Wednesday and Saturday. Or was it Tuesday and Friday? Toots was his name. He was a one-eyed fellow with a great thicket of a beard and hair down the middle of his back. You couldn't miss him. Wild-looking thing. But no one knew more about the river than he did. Hell, he'd come down it even in a spring flood when it was full of dead cows and chicken coops and moving like it was coming out of a fire hose. Why, the dam would be so far under water, it hardly made a ripple. And he'd go back up it too, although, the whole truth was, he'd be paddling back to his place way the hell across the river in what was ordinarily a man's cornfield. But, hell, he'd have to cross the river twice in order to do that. Oh, he was the man to see all right, if a fellow wanted a boat, they told him. He looked wild, but you could do business with him. As for them, the older of the fishermen said, they'd fish from, by God, shore, since neither one of them could swim a stroke.

"The hell you say," his partner protested, "I can damned well swim all kinds of strokes."

"Sure," the first one said and guffawed. He pointed out a rock to Jerry, a large flat rock about fifteen feet from the base of the dam, and explained how, early that May, his partner had fallen off that silly rock into the river and nearly beat the river dry trying to get out again.

"Maybe so," the other said, "but you saw me swim, didn't you?"

"Hell," the older fisherman insisted, "I couldn't see anything at all. It looked like an automatic car wash over there."

Both men laughed for a moment and Jerry made himself laugh with them.

"When he finally wore himself out and commenced to sink, he found out the water didn't even quite reach his tits," the older man said.

"Yes," the other said, "but I, by God, swam."

"Shit," the first said, "you didn't move a foot from where you hit the water."

"I stayed up though, damn it."

"For nearly a full minute, I'd say," the older fisherman said, "but I've seen folks swim all the way across the river and back on half as many strokes."

Jerry took the roll of Tums from his shirt pocket and tilted one into his mouth with his thumbnail. He considered the two fishermen—once behind the ear for each of them, he was thinking—*bip, bip.* He'd had all he could take of their nonsense, and the fishy, musty odor of the river was beginning to make him queasy. "I guess I better be gettin along," he told them. "Don't you fellers catch all the fish now."

"Toots," the older fisherman said. "I don't know his last name, but he's the one to see about a boat."

Jerry nodded, raised his hand, and climbed back up the steep, crooked path to where Esco slumped in the Camaro, sound asleep—one good thing about Esco, when you told him to wait, he waited, no matter how long it took, since he didn't have the imagination to do anything else.

He made Esco follow the dirt road around the dam, and they found the slough where the boats were tied. Most of them hung in the lazy current, some needing to be bailed, one or two pulled up on shore and overturned, but all of them chained to one or another of the willows along the shore. Still, it would be simple to take any of them, and many even had motors. Jerry got out of the car to look them over and found there were gas tanks aboard some of them, chained, as the motors were, to eyebolts or to the seats. But there wasn't a chain in sight that a pair of bolt cutters wouldn't take care of in a second, although it annoyed him that he'd have to waste thirty-five or forty dollars in some hardware store for the bolt cutters. He got in the car again and motioned with his forefinger for Esco to drive on. Just above the boats, they passed a launching ramp, and then the dirt road curved up a steep slope to rejoin Riverside Drive. They'd missed seeing that end of the road too, because it dropped off so steeply and because the shoulders were so grown up with weeds. "Stop at that little grocery up ahead," he told Esco. And as they bumped back up on Riverside Drive, Jerry turned to look things over so he would remember the area—it was nothing but a vacant lot, all grown up and weedy with a partially dismantled substation in the middle of it, the high-voltage signs on the fence around the substation rusty and peppered with bullet holes.

Hobb's Riverside Market was no more than fifty yards up the road, and when they pulled in, Jerry told Esco to wait in the car again.

"Come on," Esco said, "they got beer in there, and I'm thirsty and I need to get me something to eat."

Jerry pointed a finger at him. "Don't fuck me up," he said. "We came here to fish. We want to get a boat and go fishing and that's all. You got it?"

"Sure," Esco said, "I know all that."

Once inside, Esco went directly to the beer joint half of the market and ordered himself a draft and four pickled sausages. He grunted with pleasure as he bit into the first one, and he gave his head a little sideways shake and groaned loudly and happily when he finished it.

Duncan, who was sitting at the counter only a couple of stools down, turned his bleared, unfocused gaze on Esco and said matter-of-factly, "Them things'll kill ya, son. They'll eat the damned lining right out of your stomach."

"Nawh," Esco said. "I get em all the time. They're real good."

"They'll kill ya," Duncan said.

After Hobb had rung up Esco's money, he came over to see what Jerry wanted.

"Hey," Jerry said cheerfully, "I'm interested in doing a little fishing, and I want to find out about renting a boat."

"Don't rent no boats," Hobb told him.

"I know," Jerry said, trying to remember the names of the fishermen he'd met at the dam. Chadbourne was one of their names, but he couldn't remember the other. "Chadbourne and his buddy sent me up here. They said I might find a fellow named Toots who could rent me a boat or sell me one."

"Toots ain't here," Hobb said; and, apparently having decided there was no profit to be had in further conversation, he went off behind the small meat counter, ripped the top off a cardboard box, and began stamping prices on the cans inside.

Jerry struggled to maintain his dopey good cheer, but he could feel heat rising toward his ears. He ambled over to the meat counter, trying to keep the smile on his face. "I hate to trouble you, but I'd sure like to find this Toots fellow."

Hobb continued to stamp the tops of cans. "You missed him," he said. "He was in early this morning to drop off his fish, and I ain't seen him since."

"When does he usually come back?" Jerry asked.

"He could come through the door any time," Hobb said, "but he ain't due back till Monday."

"Hey, Jerry," Esco called, "this fellow says he'll rent us a boat."

Two men at a table in the corner of the room laughed at that. "Hell," one of them said, "he don't have a boat."

Duncan moved one of his elbows off the counter, rummaged in his pocket, and came out with a key ring with two keys on it, which he slid down the counter to Esco. "How about ten dollars a day?" Duncan said.

Esco shrugged and looked at Jerry, who was rigid with anger at having been called by name. "Pay him," Jerry said.

"Where the hell did you get a boat, Duncan?" one of the men at the table said, but Duncan did not reply.

"Put back any gas you run out," Duncan said. "It's tied up just above the dam."

"What's it look like?" Esco said.

"Hell, I don't know," Duncan said. "It's blue, but I ain't never laid eyes on it."

"Shit, that ain't his boat; that's his son-in-law's boat," the man at the table said. "Ha, he'll jerk a kink in your ass, Duncan, if he finds out you're rentin it on him. What if he takes a notion to go fishin?"

Duncan's bleared, disinterested gaze rested on an illuminated picture of Niagara Falls that somehow created the illusion of water in constant, violent motion. "He owes me half a year's rent," he said at last. "And anyhow, he's up and run off to Memphis."

"I saw a couple of blue boats down there," Esco said, "maybe even three of them."

Duncan sucked a tooth. "I reckon it's the one your key will unlock," he said and took a drink of his beer. "Just put it back where you got it when you're done. I'll still be warmin this stool, I expect, but you can leave the key off here even if I ain't."

Hobb looked up from his work as though to object just as Esco took a ten-dollar bill from his wallet and laid it reluctantly on the counter by Duncan's elbow. "Might as well give the money to that sour little fucker yonder so he can put it on my tab," Duncan said.

Hobb laid down his mechanical stamper at that and seemed to smooth the butcher's apron he wore with much the same satisfaction as a woman smoothing a dress she was trying on before a mirror. Without a word, he crossed the market, collected the ten-dollar bill, scribbled a note in a small thumb-worn ledger he kept below the counter, and rang the money up in his cash register.

What a pitiful excuse for a human being, Jerry was thinking. The world was full of such useless creatures, and high-grade morons who were rolling in money, and idiots like Esco. He felt hugely put upon. "Well, I guess we can go see if there are any fish in that ole river then. Thanks," he said to Duncan, who sat with his elbows propped on the counter, gazing at the illuminated beer sign, or perhaps, merely at the wall; it was hard to be sure. Duncan took a hand away from his mug of beer and raised it in lazy acknowledgment.

Later, while Esco bailed the boat and tried to get the little six-horsepower engine to run, Jerry gave himself over to a depression that had been haunting him since Sally Ann Shaw had disappeared—no, he admitted, longer than that, since it seemed clear to him now that Sally Ann had merely brought into focus what had been wrong with him all along. He knew he was intelligent. He had flair and style, but he hadn't shown the ruthlessness and daring he imagined himself to have. And if he didn't show it soon, then he was going to have to get used to being what he was at this moment, just the sort of hireling and flunky he'd always despised. "Try reading the goddamned directions for starting it," he shouted to Esco; "they're written on the goddamned motor."

"I know how to run a motor," Esco said, but he quit yanking the starting rope and leaned myopically close to the engine, scratching his head and sounding out the starting instructions.

Jerry ripped the plastic and cardboard from the two cheap rod and reel combinations they had bought at a cut-rate store and leaned them against the car. He got out the paper bag of bobbers and hooks and the small plastic fishing tackle box and set them aside, and finally, he took the Smith and Wesson from under the seat and unzipped the leather case that held it. The weight; the thin film of oil with its sweet, transparent odor; the blued perfection of its parts; the fluted silencer beside it; even the two boxes of shells he kept in the pistol case—all of it filled him with a sense of power and possibility, and reminded him, as well, of a personal failing: he was almost thirty years old, and he had never yet killed anyone.

He flipped the cylinder to the side, assured himself that it was loaded, and flipped it shut. Carefully he screwed the silencer on the barrel and found, just as he suspected, that the pistol would no longer fit inside the tackle box. He'd known when he'd bought all the silly fishing props that he would need a larger box, but he had begrudged such a waste of money. He took the silencer off again, put everything back in the pistol case, and closed the case inside the tackle box. Down at the river, the little outboard engine sputtered, caught, and died, but before Jerry got the car closed up and locked, Esco had it running.

Under way at last, Jerry tried to convince himself they were on something more than a fool's errand, but there was a little knot of despair in the pit of his stomach that argued otherwise. This fellow, Toots, was a strong lead, but even if he should happen to have seen her, the chances that he could tell them anything that might help them track her down seemed ridiculously slim. Too much time had passed; she could have traveled too far. Maybe, if he could spend six months or a year looking for her, he might find her. Maybe not. More than likely they'd seen the last of Sally Ann Shaw. And what a useless, silly spectacle the two of them would be making of themselves if she were in Miami or New York City or San Francisco or any one of a thousand other places they might never even dream of. But as much as it shamed him, as much as it infuriated him, some part of him would be secretly pleased if they never saw her again, if only because it would serve Roland right, if only because it would prove that some simple bitch off the street could do what he should have done himself a long time ago. He'd thought about it often, but he'd never quite planned it out, never quite moved it out of the realm of bitter, ambitious day-dreams. He'd thought he'd been serious about it, but some-how she'd called his bluff and taught him otherwise. This very morning, for the first time, he'd begun to assess oppor-tunity carefully. He'd been alone with Esco and the money only in the car and in the elevator of the Maxwell House Hotel. But he could hardly shoot a man who was driving him around on the streets of Nashville in broad daylight, and to shoot him in an elevator that might stop at any floor and present him with half a dozen witnesses was madness. Once they were in the hotel room all reasonable opportunity was lost; taking on three men with a twenty-two pistol was far too risky. No doubt either the Texan or the Puerto Rican was armed. Probably both. Although what a play it would be to have the money and the coke too. Still, there was no telling how well connected those two might be, and Billy Wayne wasn't connected at all. No, the thing had to be planned. He had to have Esco or Billy Wayne alone, and he had to have his getaway worked out carefully. But he'd do it. He knew he'd do it now and soon. The risks merely had to be small enough to be acceptable. It would be stupid and bush to make a move otherwise, and he was neither.

He turned around and motioned for Esco to cut the engine so he could explain one more time who was going to do the talking and who was going to keep his mouth shut when they found this Toots fellow. "I want us to be real friendly with this hick, right?" Jerry said.

"Right," Esco repeated.

"Now if I should get the idea he's keeping anything from us, then I'll turn you loose, and you can do what you want. But not till I say so."

"Right," Esco said again and seemed to puff himself up like a frog getting ready to croak.

It took nearly nothing, Jerry decided, to make Esco feel happy and important, but Christ, he'd always felt strangely ridiculous when he talked to him, as though he were trying to hold a conversation with a diesel truck. Esco twisted the throttle, the bow of the boat lifted slightly, and they were under way again, although they generated a great deal more noise than speed. Jerry propped up the fishing rods so they'd be clearly visible, watched the red and white bobbers clipped to their lines vibrate to the labors of the motor, watched the monotonous banks of the river crawl by, and tried to endure the knot of ill will and despair that rode in his stomach. He had to grip the gunnels and grind his teeth in order to keep from admitting that he was either a coward or a fool, since he knew perfectly well he could have taken Billy Wayne's money that very morning. He could have shoved his pistol against Esco's ribs and made him drive out into the country, put a bullet through that dull brain of his, taken the money and gone anywhere he liked just the way Sally Ann had. Hell, he wouldn't even have had to do that. Halfway to the Maxwell House Hotel, he could have convinced Esco to stop off at a drugstore to pick up a prescription for Roland. Esco wasn't any smarter than a ball peen hammer and wouldn't have seen through it, and when he'd bullied him out of the car and into the store, he could have simply driven off with the money. By the time Esco figured out what had happened and called Roland, he could have been in his own car and headed west. He'd simply had a failure of guts and imagination all along, even this morning; and he could no longer excuse himself for phony reasons. He had to quit pretending he saw no proper opportunities, or make up his mind that he was no better than Esco.

As they came around a bend, and another monotonous stretch of river revealed itself, he noticed at the far end of it a small cluster of boats nosed into shore. Perhaps, he thought, they belonged to Toots. Perhaps he could find this silly bastard quickly, ask a few questions he felt beforehand would yield absolutely nothing of value, and get himself off this suffocating, sweltering river. He had, by God, bigger fish to fry. He would make a plan, and he would execute it, and Mr. Billy Wayne Roland would find himself stung a second time. When they drew closer to the boats, he motioned for Esco to slow down and began to look for some sort of tree house. Was it supposed to be out over the water or what?

He was looking up into the treetops, moving his head this way and that, trying to see around the foliage, when he saw her. He saw her before he saw the tree house she was in. He saw her through the window in profile, but she was turning in their direction. "Go on," he whispered fiercely to Esco. "Go on, damn it." But Esco only looked confused and kept the throttle exactly where it was, apparently not realizing he had been expected to stop in the first place. "Look over there," Jerry said and pointed across the river, so Esco would turn his face away from the tree house and Sally Ann. "Look there and there," Jerry said and kept pointing, and Esco kept looking, his face a picture of bland, mindless puzzlement, as though sooner or later he'd see what Jerry wanted him to see but wouldn't be much interested when he did. When they had gone another hundred yards and around another bend, Jerry had him pull into shore. "Goddamn!" he said. "Goddamn if I didn't see her! I looked right at her!"

"Who?" Esco said.

# 13

She watched him as he lay sleeping on the bunk as though he were the sole survivor of a shipwreck. All his bones seemed far too large for him—the ribbed vault of his chest and the rough bowl of his pelvis, his knee joints and elbows, his wrists and ankles. Somehow he looked as if he'd gone through a great ordeal and lost flesh. Yet he looked strong too. What wasn't bone seemed all lean muscle and stubborn sinew. To the waist his skin was brown and tough as leather. Below, his groin, his pale ropy penis, his thighs and calves, and even his large misshapen feet with their toes rotated so oddly to the side—that half of him was nearly as white as milk. She'd had many lovers, but never a two-toned one, never one that looked like this. Maybe, she thought, he'd been prettier in his day, although it was difficult for her to guess when his day might have been. Still, he had looked right dashing with his new clothes on.

She made a small bemused sound in her throat and shook her head: he was no candidate for a pinup poster for sure, but there was something about him nevertheless, some bizarre appeal as though he were a rough sketch that hadn't been fleshed out, or a caricature, or better yet, as though he had been whittled from a stubborn knotty wood that had made its own demands on the finished product; whatever, there was a certain ungainly, clownish sort of dignity about him. But he wasn't the man a girl would dream about, particularly a girl like herself who had always taken a secret pride in the physical beauty of her lovers, whatever other faults they might have had.

She'd been so occupied with Toots, she'd been hearing it

for some moments before she realized what it was. Motorboats made her nervous every time they happened by, but this one seemed to be coming from up the river, and somehow, if trouble came by boat, she expected it to come the other way. The devil of it was that she'd been fooled before in this matter of direction. Maybe it was the nature of the way sound traveled over water, or perhaps the bluff distorted things or made some sort of echo. Yet she was certain this one was coming downstream and watched anxiously for it to appear, unaware that she was holding her breath.

But, at last, she saw that it too had fooled her and was coming up from town. It had got past the little opening in the trees by the time she realized her mistake. Still, the few intermittent glimpses she got of it through the thick screen of leaves comforted her. She got a peek of fishing poles and red and white bobbers, and anyway, the two people aboard appeared to be interested in something across the river and didn't even glance toward the tree house. She let her breath out and looked again at Toots, who hadn't even stirred, and the smile she gave him was warm, affectionate, almost motherly in its small taint of condescension. She felt she had annexed him somehow. Naturalized him. It was a feeling both happy and sad, as though she had taught a wild bird to eat from her palm. Even the tree house seemed far less strange. It was only a house in a tree after all. And Toots, even Toots, was only himself. It was as if she'd entered some barbarous territory and tamed it to her purpose, domesticated it, made it familiar and comfortable and chased all its myths away. That's the way she'd felt about making love to men ever since she'd been a young girl. She'd never quite known how to treat them, never quite known what to say or do, until she'd made love to them. It cut through the strained, coy perjury of flirtation. It got the big troublesome question—will we or won't we—out of the way. But more than that it naturalized them or normalized them or neutralized them or exorcised them or something—all, anyway, except that goddamned Billy Wayne Roland.

Oh God, she thought, was that really the way she had lived, was that really her secret agenda? And what on earth did it have to do with her vision of being dressed all in white, having spring flowers braided into her hair, standing on a huge empty stage and singing of love, a single spotlight upon her like the gentle blessing of the moon? Jesus Christ, she thought, the grand illusion and the secret agenda. May Morning and Sally Ann Shaw. Which one, she wondered, had betrayed her more?

Phooey, she thought, what kind of thinking was that? Neither one had done her in. Here she was, alive and well, hail and hearty. The only problem she had, the one and only problem, was to decide how she wanted to live the rest of her life. And she had a whole sackful of money to help her along. If she took a notion, she could buy a new Mercedes to drive around in while she thought the matter over. Or maybe she'd take a cruise on one of those fancy luxury liners; that could certainly help a girl consider her options. Who could tell, maybe she could get a job singing right there on board. Or maybe she'd become an airline stewardess. A business woman. She could even go to college if she wanted. Become a poet. Or a painter, say. She'd always liked drawing in school. So why was she so down and blue?

But she was as down and blue as she had ever been. She fingered the new clothes Toots had bought her where they lay half out of their boxes on the tabletop. She ran her hand over them, straightened a collar here, fluffed a pleat there. Oh, but Toots had been a gentle and considerate lover, and Billy Wayne's rape hadn't really hurt her, and Toots hadn't hurt her, so why did she ache? It hurt around her heart, or anyway what was happening was almost pain; for sure it was a terrible, sad, labored feeling, as though its valves were squeaking each time it beat. And she felt heavy in her bones too, as though if she fell in the river she'd sink like lead, as though she could only move in slow motion, only creep about like an old woman. She'd begun to have the feeling even while Toots was making love to her, as if, having given him permission, having given any number of lovers permission, made her wonder if she hadn't given Billy Wayne permission; somehow made her wonder if she hadn't deserved what he had done to her. God knows, more than once in her life this matter of permission had been open to question; the line wasn't always so easy to draw. And how would he have behaved if she'd been a different sort of woman, a woman of great virtue and purity, say? God, she thought, what nonsense, what rot. The son of a bitch had raped her and that was that. What could she be thinking? Could a girl only decide to be a virgin or a whore? What total rot! It wasn't at all fair that her heart should ache as though she were in some devious way at fault.

She wouldn't have it. He had raped her, and she had his money, and she was going to make a new life with it. She would have to ignore the feeling that she didn't know how to make a new life, that she knew how to be a waitress and she knew how to dream about being a big singing star and that was all. Oh, she could work in a mill or be a checkout girl in a supermarket, but that was the same as being a waitress. For sure and certain, she didn't know how to be rich. She had no notion how to deal with money. Being poor was something she could handle, get her teeth into; it came with a whole set of worries one could count on like bothersome, faithful friends. Worst of all, the money she had was tainted. It had nothing of the solid feel of money she'd earned herself. It had lost its character, weight, and value. Besides, taking it from Billy Wayne had made her feel dirty and implicated as though she'd put a price on being raped. Jesus, was that the logic here—did everything with her have its price? *Well, let's see, fellow, for regular sex with consent and permission? Hmmm, that will cost you a certain amount of charm, a little kindness and attention, and reasonable good looks. Want it kinky? Let's see, that calls for the proper atmosphere, perhaps a little alcohol or some decent dope to loosen up the old inhibitions, and some serious attention to foreplay. What's that? Rape, you say? Well then, that's more expensive. What? With beating, name calling, miscellaneous pain, cruelty, degrada-*

*tion, and buggering? Oh my, that's close to the top of the line—you see, we don't quite know yet what the top of the line might be—but sure, we can let you have all that; it's on special this week for a quarter of a million and change.* Merciful Jesus, she thought, was she going nuts or what? Maybe, she thought, maybe she was. And maybe she was simply going to die of the strange affliction around her heart that was growing more painful by the minute. She felt cold, despite the fact she guessed the temperature was close to ninety. And she felt very lonely. She looked again at Toots, lying all helter-skelter on the narrow little bunk as if he had fallen there from some great height. He was on his back, one arm flung over his head behind him, the other, which she had been lying upon, which had cradled her, bent so that his hand rested gently against his chest just where she'd put it when she'd risen, pulled on her slip, and begun to torture herself with all sorts of silly thoughts.

She wanted him awake. All of a sudden she felt incapable of being alone, and she got up from her chair, knelt by his bunk, and stroked his cheek with the back of her hand.

He smiled in his sleep and flexed his toes like an infant.

She took hold of his chin and shook it gently. "Hey," she said. "Hey, you gonna sleep the rest of the afternoon?"

His blue eye opened, blinked once, and seemed, in the very next moment, to pore over her with great sobriety as if he hadn't been asleep at all.

"Huh?" she said, "you gonna stay in bed the rest of the day?"

"Well," he said, "it's an interesting notion, and I'm giving it some thought."

"Ha," she said. "Ain't you the least little bit hungry? It must be nearly six o'clock, and you haven't had nothin since breakfast."

"No," he said, "I'm not hungry." He took her face and cupped it between his rough hands, and she could see a tiny image of herself in his eye like a photograph secreted away in a locket. She felt suddenly so drawn to him she found herself climbing up onto the narrow bunk to be held. Still, the tribulation around her heart persisted, although she held him close in order to drive it out. She didn't know exactly what sort of remedy she expected to take from him, perhaps only the comfort a child might take from a father, or merely the mild solace of being close to another human being. And it did seem to help. But the oddest and most illogical part was that, exactly to the same degree it helped, it made the feeling worse. And then too she could feel his prick growing and warming up until it was hard and hot against her thigh. Ha, she thought, had she really expected to get in bed with a man and hold him and have it not come to this?

"I don't know . . ." he said and then he stopped. "I mean it wasn't so long ago that you . . ." he said and stopped again. "I wouldn't want to hurt . . ." he said.

"Shhh," she said, "hush up," and, as though she were very tired, she pushed herself upright and pulled the slip off over her head.

"I mean, isn't this . . ." he said.

"Hush now," she said and lay down with him again, her bruised cheek against the knobby bones of his shoulder until he raised her face to kiss her damaged eye and cheek and mouth. It felt very good after all. Who could say it wasn't a healing touch and couldn't restore what had been taken away? In some remote station of her brain she wasn't even sure any longer exactly when the real damage had been done; maybe it had been cumulative somehow, and that son of a bitch Billy Wayne had merely shocked her awake, showed her something she couldn't fail to see. Oh, she decided, she was beginning to have crazy thoughts again, but she would push them away. She kissed his flat, rough nipple, the sparse grizzled hair around it springy as wire; she kissed the shaved and shiny hinge of his jaw still flavored with after-shave lotion. She moved again so that she could offer him her own breasts to suck, and when he took a nipple into his mouth, a great melting warmth seemed to enter her there and spread along some strange, tingling network that seemed to connect everything from the roots of her hair to her toes. His hands cupped her breasts, smoothed her flanks and hips, enveloped her buttocks. and she moved to cover that part of him which was rigid and full of velvet heat. Ha, she thought. Ha. If she tried, if she really tried, if she turned herself wrong side out, she might be able to rid herself of what was hurting her and replace it with something else that was comforting and whole and would last. Oh my, she thought, it was worth a try anyway—oh yes, it was, it was, it was, it was.

# 14

All bets are off, Jerry was thinking as he slipped the Smith and Wesson inside the bellyband of his trousers. He pulled his T-shirt out so that the pistol was hidden, tucked the silencer into his left front pocket and a box of shells into his hip pocket. His mouth was dry as tinder with excitement, and he licked his lips. "Chain the boat around that tree, lock it, and give me the key," he told Esco.

"I'm the one responsible for it," Esco said. "I'm the one he rented it to."

Jerry put the pistol case back in the tackle box and set the tackle box in the bow of the boat while Esco wrapped the chain around a maple and locked it. He didn't know what the rest of the day might require of him, but he wanted the key in his pocket. He held his hand out to Esco and wiggled his fingers until Esco dropped it reluctantly into his palm. If he had to shoot him, he didn't want to have to search through all his pockets for any damned key.

"I wasn't going to lose it," Esco said.

"Look," Jerry said, "Roland told me if we got his money back and if you did a good job, there'd be a two-thousand-dollar bonus in it for you. But you'll want to do everything I tell you exactly when I tell you to do it."

"I always do a good job," Esco said with dignity. "Nobody can say I don't."

"That's right," Jerry said. "You're a real professional, and I know you won't let me down this time either. I know I can count on you to do what needs to be done, even if it's tough."

"Right," Esco said, although he looked a little unsure, as

if he wondered if the conversation hadn't turned on him somehow, wondered if what appeared to be a compliment wasn't some sort of clever way for Jerry to lord it over him.

"Now," Jerry said, "we need to be careful. We don't want anybody to know we're around until we're ready, so we've got to go slow and be quiet and stay out of sight. We've got to look things over. Probably we won't do anything at all until it gets dark, but we don't want to give them a chance to run."

It was his fate to have that quarter of a million, Jerry thought; what else could explain that dumb bitch hanging around? His mouth was so dry he couldn't gather enough moisture to swallow properly. Even his tongue was dry and failed to moisten his lips when he licked them. He was going to have to get hold of himself.

He couldn't believe it. Something had to go wrong. Surely she'd passed the money off to someone else. It couldn't be so easy as this. But maybe it was. God knows she was no trouble to find. Perhaps this Toots fellow was a relative or something. Likely he was, and probably the stupid bitch still had the money right with her. It was possible she was no smarter than Esco. The world was full of stupid people. His only problem was simply realizing how stupid they were and taking proper advantage of it. Yes, he thought, that had always been his problem. It was hard to believe that people were really as gullible and thick and dull-witted as they appeared. If he could have believed how trusting most dumb bastards were, he could have walked off with half the world by now. "Stay a little more behind me and watch where the hell you put your feet down," he told Esco. "You sound like a goddamned elephant." He wiped some of the sweat from his face with his curled forefinger and conveyed the moisture to his mouth—salty as it was, it was at least wet. He was going to have to be cool. He was going to have to be as efficient and merciless as a machine. First he had to have the money in his possession. Esco would be good for that since he could squeeze any information out of anybody. Then he'd have to kill Sally Ann and this Toots fellow. He didn't know how Esco would take that, but he wouldn't give him a chance to object. *Bip, bip.* One, two, and it would be done; and then Esco wouldn't have much choice but to do what was needed. Probably it wouldn't bother him anyway. Not much did. Then he'd have to get rid of the bodies, which would be easy, since he could weight them down and sink them in the river. Esco would be good for that too. He could have Esco paddle them downriver a hundred yards or so from the tree house and drop them overboard. They could use one of the boats pulled up on shore. While Esco was gone, he himself could gather some rope and weights. It would be best to shoot him just as he pulled into the shore. That way, he'd already be in the boat, and the fat son of a bitch wouldn't have to be dragged or carried anywhere. He could weight him down where he lay, paddle him out into the river and sink his ass as well. Then he'd only have to motor back to town, chain the boat up where they'd found it, and return the key. No, he wouldn't return the key. It was best not to be seen any more often than necessary—he'd throw the fucking key in the river. As long as the boat was back where it belonged, no one would make a fuss. Then, by God, he could get in the car and drive away free as a bird and rich as a bastard. What could Billy Wayne do? Call the police? Hell no, he couldn't do anything. Not one god-damned thing. Nothing. And anyway, for all Billy Wayne would know, he and Esco might have bought it. All by herself Sally Ann Shaw had sure put his dick in a sling.

Off in the leafy distance he saw a corner of a small building and got a glimpse of the underpinnings of the tree house. He motioned Esco up beside him and shushed him. Just this side of the scrappy clearing around the tree house there was a brush pile, and he pointed it out to Esco. "There," he whispered, "we'll hide behind that until dark. Go slow," he said. "We don't want to make a sound between here and there." He drew his pistol, swung the cylinder out to make sure it was loaded, and screwed on the silencer, which made the pistol ungainly and barrel heavy, but also made it seem doubly potent as though it might possess its own deadly volition. Jerry's tongue was so dry it seemed to rattle and click against his lips when he tried to lick them, and even Esco seemed unmanned by the sight of the pistol, although he didn't say a word. Still, Jerry thought he saw Esco's ignorant pride in his own strength seem to retreat and leave him a little less smug. Jerry stuck the pistol once more inside the waist of his trousers; the cold steel of the silencer reached all the way down into his pubic hair and made him feel strange.

By the time they reached the pile of slash at the edge of the clearing, Jerry had begun to tremble and his knees had turned a little watery. "All right," he told Esco in a breathy whisper, "this is where we stay till dark." It would be risky, he thought, to try to cross the twenty-five or thirty yards of relatively cleared land to the tree house in broad daylight. What if someone up there had a shotgun? Hell, any sort of gun? He was nearly certain they hadn't been seen, but the chances were good they would be if they tried to cross the clearing before dark, and even if they weren't shot down in the process, even if they got under the tree house where they'd be pretty safe, they would have given themselves away. He looked at the ladder which rose from the ground to the narrow little porch running around the tree house and shook his head. It would be suicidal to try to climb up that damned thing if anyone up there knew you were coming. No, he thought, there was nothing to be done except to wait and keep watch until dark.

His angle of vision wasn't very good, but he couldn't see anyone inside the tree house. He could see a dim hint of ceiling and back wall through the screen door, but the screen itself put a haze across his vision, and the house was dim inside. He considered the narrow catwalk running along the bluff to a pipe from which a steady stream of water flowed —spring water, no doubt; Christ, he'd give fifty dollars to be able to drink his fill from it—but it didn't look possible to climb up to the catwalk; it was a good twenty feet from the ground up the sheer face of the bluff, and anyway, the approach from the catwalk to the tree house would be even more exposed and dangerous. It looked just possible to climb down to the roof of the tree house from above. The upper part of the bluff looked ledgy and tufted with a few scrubby bushes and stunted trees one might hang on to, but landing on the roof like Santa Claus and his reindeer didn't seem too smart. No, the best plan was still to wait until dark, sneak up the ladder, and take them by surprise. How many of them were there? He hadn't seen anyone but Sally Ann, but there could be three or four tough bastards up there with her, and him with nothing more than a twenty-two pistol. He'd feel a lot better if Esco had a gun. His mouth was dry as tinder, and he could feel himself vibrating like a tuning fork. He had to get himself in hand. He had the brains, and he had the element of surprise. That ought to be enough, he thought. All he had to do was be cool and completely without mercy. Nonsense, he thought, he'd never felt the slightest touch of mercy. This was no time to delude himself. It was the turning point of his whole life. He had to be without fear. That was the point. He had to be fucking fearless. This business of mercy was a hoax, a flimsy ruse; he'd never even understood what the word meant; he'd never once felt its presence, wasn't even sure it existed, and, therefore, couldn't accept it as a reason for failure. He either had the balls or he didn't.

He glanced at Esco, who was leaning against the brush pile, facing the way they'd come, his eyelids drooping and his gaze unfocused. The son of a bitch was only minutes away from nodding off to sleep. Incredible! The simple bastard was going to take a nap! Well, so much the better. He went back to watching the tree house. No wires coming in, which meant no phone. Good. But there didn't seem to be anyone moving around up there, and not a sound. Suppose —the thought drew his stomach into a knot—suppose Sally Ann had seen them and recognized them, and while they were going on upriver and then creeping back again, she had slipped away a second time. Suppose he and Esco were stalking an empty house? He raised his head enough to look at the boats tied along the shore. They looked the same, but the trouble was he hadn't bothered to count them and so couldn't quite tell if one was missing. He didn't think so, but he couldn't be sure. And perhaps they hadn't left by boat anyway. Goddamn, he thought, goddamn, what if it wasn't his fate to get the quarter of a million, but to play the fool over and over again? His stomach tightened and began to burn and he reached into his shirt pocket for a Tums. His mouth was so dry the tablet turned to dust under his teeth, and he nearly drew the dust into his lungs. He did not wish to cough, even though he wasn't at all sure it would matter if he did. He pressed the chalky powder against his soft palate with his tongue and tried his best to gather enough moisture in his mouth to swallow it. After a minute or two he got most of it down, and the bile rising in his throat retreated. He deserved the money. He'd earned it by virtue of all the aggravation he'd suffered, but he knew damned good and well that silly bitch had made another getaway. Esco had dropped off to sleep, and he gazed at him, not so much seeing Esco as the grim aspect of his own foolishness and failure.

When the screen door of the tree house slapped shut, he almost jumped out of his skin, and even Esco opened his eyes and began to stir, but he put a hand on Esco's shoulder and shushed him. A man wearing absolutely nothing at all came out along the catwalk. He was carrying a bucket. Carefully Jerry drew his pistol but decided at once not to use it. It would have been nice to cut the odds by one, but the distance was too far, and anyway, even if his aim were true, the man might cry out, or whoever was in the treehouse might hear him fall, even if they didn't notice, and they wouldn't, the small spitting sound the pistol would make. The man didn't appear to be the hermit the fisherman at the dam had described; there was no long hair, no beard. Perhaps Toots was in the house with Sally Ann. Jesus, he thought, what sort of cheap, kinky bitch was she? He didn't understand any of it. Why would anyone steal a quarter of a million dollars and then run off to live in a fucking crummy pigsty in the middle of the woods? The world was full of lunatics. He watched the man drink from his cupped palms, watched him splash water on his face and chest, watched him fill his bucket while the inside of his own throat felt suddenly as though it were made of cracked boot leather. He would have loved to step out and confront the man. It filled him with a kind of insane glee to imagine how vulnerable the man would feel to be caught naked as the day he was born while someone held a pistol aimed at his balls. But he did not move and was rewarded with the sight of a Band-Aid over one of the man's eyes. The eye looked sunken and sealed, the skull around it, cadaverous. This Toots fellow, he decided, must have cleaned up his act. Sure he had; he'd come into a bunch of money. And he'd bet Sally Ann was up there with him alone—sure, she wasn't very likely to be into some kinky sort of group sex. He decided to shoot Toots at once and deal with Sally Ann at his convenience, and he raised his pistol to take aim, but he was trembling, and the man was too far, and he couldn't be sure of the shot. No, he decided, his original plan was best. It was a perfect plan. He watched Toots go back along the catwalk, his ass shining like two pieces of white rice tacked to a board, and he almost laughed out loud with happiness.

# 15

Even though he'd never met so complicated a creature as Sally Ann Shaw, even though it was like looking at a kaleidoscope to witness her moods and whims, he was bewitched. How many women, he wondered, could she be? More frightening yet, how many men, he wondered, could he?

"What I wouldn't give for a shower," she said when he came through the door. "A long, long shower."

"The river's not so bad," he told her. "It's a little warm on top, but you can swim down until you find the right temperature."

"Not me," she said. "I'm not a swimmer, and even if I were, I don't want a bunch of wildlife taking a bath with me—frogs and catfish and turtles and snakes—no thanks," she said and twitched her shoulders as if she were shaking some such creature from her back. "I don't even like rubber ducks." She was wearing her slip again and setting some of her new clothes aside on a chair. "But, hey, it'll be great to put on something clean for a change, and a sponge bath is better than nothing." She gave her head a slight tilt, and the corners of her mouth turned up. "But wouldn't it be grand to get a real nice motel room somewhere, eat dinner in a dynamite resturant, and then go dancing or something? Jesus," she said wistfully, "even just to see a movie?"

He went out on the catwalk, pumped up the Coleman stove, lit it, and set the bucket of water over the flame. Inside again, he felt suddenly embarrassed by his nakedness and pawed down through the old clothes he'd worn to town until he found his trousers, which he put on with his back to her.

He dragged a second bucket from under the sideboard; got a nail from a coffee can; a hammer from his toolbox in the cave; and, turning the bucket upside down, knocked five holes in the bottom.

"What in the world are you doing?" she asked.

"Making a shower," he said.

He set the galvanized wash tub over the trap door and studied the eyebolt in the roof beam. He considered a coil of rope hanging from a peg in the wall, but shook his head and went off into the cave again. When he came back, he'd bent the nail into a crude *C*, and he attached the handle of the bucket to the eyebolt with it. "There," he said. "I guess if you soap up before you use it, there'll be enough water to rinse you anyhow."

"Thank you," she said.

He took a chair from under the table and set it by the tub so she could stand on its seat to pour the water in, and then, plucking the end of his nose thoughtfully, he stood back to consider his creation. It took him only a moment to realize the shower served no earthly purpose whatever. It made very little difference whether she stood in a tub and reached down for water or had it dripping on her from a bucket hung over her head. What she wanted, he realized with sudden clarity, was tile around her and porcelain and chrome. She wished for thick bath mats and towels, fluorescent lights, a proper mirror, and the sort of water that rushed instantly from one shiny fixture and disappeared almost as quickly into another and in the meantime could accommodate the slightest whim concerning its temperature and force. It made him blush to realize what a bad joke his shower was. "If we got dressed and took off right now, we could get to town by dark or a little after," he told her. "There's a real fancy motel over on the Nashville highway."

"I was just being silly," she said. "I'm not ready to go public yet. And anyway, how would it look for us to come walking up to some fancy place on foot and without a sign of luggage? And the money! Jesus, we'd have to drag all that money along with us in that silly laundry sack. No thanks! But, hey, you don't have to make such a long face about it," she said, laughing and putting her arms around him. "What are you looking so sad about, for Christ's sake?"

"We could take a taxi," he told her, "and no one's going to bother your money. No one's ever bothered this place in all the years . . ."

"I'm not ready yet," she told him, and he could feel another change coming over her; he could feel it in the way she held him.

"All right," he said.

"I just don't know what to do," she said. "I always used to know what to do. Right or wrong, I could at least make up my mind. I didn't even have to give it any thought. Christ," she said, and he felt a tiny explosion of miserable laughter against his shoulder, "I'd just take a notion and bang, I'd do it. Good or bad, right or wrong. But I feel like I've been canceled out some way or other. I mean I had plans," she said. "I knew who the hell I was and what I was up to. I was used to myself, you know, like when you get used to a pair of shoes. You might want a fancy new pair, but . . . oh shit . . . what am I going to do?"

"What do you want to do?" he asked her.

"I want you to hold on to me," she said.

"All right," he told her.

"That son of a bitch just canceled me out someway."

"No he didn't," he told her, not having any idea what the truth of the matter might be, but feeling called upon to argue.

"I was so mad at first I just didn't notice that he took my whole life away."

He wondered if that were true, or if she merely thought it was. He wondered if the distinction mattered. He thought of suggesting that losing her old life might be a good thing. Well, he could tell her, you're just another born-again

Christian. It might make her laugh. But it might not. There was a pretty serious difference in the initiation after all. He petted the nape of her neck and kept his mouth shut.

An enormous, wet sigh fluttered across his breastbone, and she said, "I want my bath," and pushed herself from the circle of his arms.

"Sure," he said. He went out on the catwalk and stuck his finger in the bucket of water. "It's only just barely warm," he told her.

"That's all right," she said. "That's just fine."

He brought her water in and set it on the table, remembering with disappointment that he hadn't given a single thought to her supper. He could have bought a bottle of wine when he was in town, picked up some beef, say, or a chicken. A chicken, seasoned, wrapped in tinfoil, and covered in a thick layer of clay from the riverbank, nearly always cooked very well in the firepit he'd dug beside his garden, but the process took nearly all afternoon. Now and again in the warm months, when firing up the wood stove would make the camp unbearable, he fixed himself a chicken in such a way. He was going to have to take more thought about such matters now that she was with him; he couldn't continue to be so mindlessly omnivorous—six or eight tomatoes picked from the vine for supper one night, a catfish the next, nothing the third, perhaps a half a jar of pickles and a pan of homefries on the fourth. He was going to have to get himself in hand. Suddenly adream, he pondered what it would take to move his camp a little way toward the twentieth century. He could put in a bathroom, a kitchen sink, electricity. And, he wondered, did they still have those dance studios where a fellow could go and maybe pick up a few steps? In some remote corner of his brain perhaps he knew how ludicrous and absurd such gestures would be, but he didn't know he knew it, for he was only aware of a strange feeling in his stomach as though he were on the long downward arc of some carnival ride.

"Hey," she said, "weren't you gonna go jump in the river or something?"

"I was just thinking . . ." he said and waved a hand around helplessly, "I was just getting ready to ask what you'd like for supper."

She had collected one of his threadbare towels and a piece of soap, and she set them on the bunk next to the tub. "I'm not very hungry," she said. "I'm not sure I want anything."

Somehow he wasn't very hungry himself. "Soup," he said, "how about a little soup?"

"Sure," she said.

He began to look over his small store of canned goods on the shelves above the sideboard when he realized the light was very poor. It would be totally dark by the time he got back from the river. He lit two kerosene lamps and set one on the table for her and used the other to help him see the labels of cans. He had peaches, pears, lima beans, spam, sardines, but no damned soup. It made him feel defeated and sad. Finally, pushing cans this way and that, he discovered a single dusty can of beef stew. "How about some stew and some peaches?" he said.

"Sure," she said, "that's just fine."

"I don't have any soup," he confessed and rubbed the back of his neck apologetically.

"That's okay. That's just fine," she said.

All at once he understood that she was waiting patiently for him to leave. She wanted to bathe, after all, and she wouldn't want him standing around like some halfwit, watching her.

"Well then, I guess I'll be back after a while," he told her, and grabbing up a small piece of soap from the sideboard, he took himself through the door and out on the catwalk.

He was just about to start down the ladder when he realized it was already occupied. Someone was coming up. "Hey," Toots said, surprised but not unfriendly, "what can I do for you?"

"Back the fuck up and put your hands on your head!" the stranger said.

At least that's what it sounded like; Toots wasn't at all certain he'd understood properly since he was getting ready to ask the man to climb back down the ladder—it would be better, he thought, to find out what this fellow wanted when they were both on the ground and out of Sally Ann's way. He had even turned protectively back toward the tree house to make sure Sally Ann was still decent before the man's strange greeting got through to him. "What?" he asked, turning back around, but already shocked a second time by the glimpse he'd gotten of Sally Ann, who was frozen in the act of taking off her slip, her eyes startled and round with fear.

"Shut up and don't move!" the man said. He was head and shoulders above the catwalk, trying to hold on to a rung and point some strange device at Toots. He rose yet another rung and opened his mouth to say something else, but he never got it said because an incredible glut of water pounded through the screen, hit him full in the face, and seemed to strangle him.

Toots would have saved him if he could. He tried, but the ladder was far too vertical to accommodate such a startled reaction, and when the man recoiled, the ladder went with him, and Toots couldn't grab it in time.

The ladder fell, and, framed between two rungs like a portrait of hysteria, the man's wet face fell away with it. And the rope, tied to the top rung of the ladder, made the pulley over Toots' head sing. Just before the ladder hit, the knot at the end of the rope jammed into the pulley, and the ladder stopped at an acute angle, but the man kept going to hit the hardpacked mud around the base of the tree house with an awful smack.

"Pull the ladder up! Pull the ladder up!" Sally Ann shouted, already through the door, out on the catwalk with him, and jumping up and down trying to reach the pulley and free the rope.

"Jesus, I think he might be dead," Toots muttered, looking at the man on the ground.

"Help me!" Sally Ann shouted, beating his back with her fists and weeping. "It's them! It's them!" But she gave up on him almost at once and began hauling the ladder up by the rope, hand over hand, until at last he became aware of her frenzied labor and helped her pull the ladder up on the catwalk.

"That's what's his name? That's Roland?" Toots asked her, looking down at the man who had begun, at last, to twitch in a frantic, herky-jerky sort of way.

"Get inside, for God's sake, before they shoot us!" Sally Ann cried and pulled on his arm.

Another man had appeared out of the shadowy dark and, after a moment's indecision, began to drag the first one under the tree house as Sally Ann pulled Toots off the catwalk and back through the door. The man who had fallen was making a noise like a hinge that needed oiling: "Eeeeeeeeee. Eeeeeeeeee. Eeeeeeee," he went.

"Oh God," Sally Ann said, "what are we going to do? I knew he'd find me. I knew he would. We're dead for certain."

Beneath the floor of the tree house, the man who had fallen went, "Eeeeeeeeeee. Eeeeeeeeeee. Eeeeeeeeuuuuuh."

Toots shook his head in disbelief.

"That nasty little shit who was getting ready to shoot you works for Billy Wayne," Sally Ann said through her tears, "and so does that other moron who dragged him away." Sally Ann bent toward the floor and clenched her fists. "You better get away from here right now, or we'll shoot you full of holes!" she screamed.

"Eeeeuuuuh. Eeeuuuuuh. Uhhhhhhhhhh," the man under the tree house said.

"Haven't you got any sort of gun?" Sally Ann whispered, her eyes wild and her face streaming with tears.

Toots shook his head, realizing that the fellow she had drenched with her bath water had, indeed, been pointing a pistol at him, a pistol with a silencer, for Christ's sake. He'd seen them in gangster movies back when he was in high school.

"Oh God," Sally Ann said and wrung her hands, "how can we get out of here?"

"We're all right," Toots told her. "I don't believe they can get up to us." He reached out to take hold of her and calm her, but she pulled away and stamped her foot on the floor.

"You better get away from here! Right now!" she screamed. "We've already called the police!" But her voice was ripped and ragged with weeping and couldn't have fooled anyone.

# 16

Jerry was so chastened, he could only sit with his back propped against a tree, shaking head to foot. Each cell in his body felt pricked with pins and needles, but at least he could breathe again, although the process felt raw and tenuous.

The laws of nature had gone mad, totally mad. Only a berserk partiality could have made him the victim. It was outrageous to attack an armed man with a bucket of water. You threw a bucket of water on dogs fucking on your lawn, but not on a man armed with a pistol who clearly had the upper hand. And the ladder, it had taken that son of a bitching ladder all week to fall, and yet the ground had smacked into him so suddenly and with such violence, it knocked the last molecule of air from his lungs, punished his kidneys, addled his brain, and hammered his spine to near paralysis. You just couldn't fall with such agonizing slowness and hit so brutally hard. And wasn't nature supposed to abhor a vacuum? So why couldn't he breathe? So why didn't air simply rush into his lungs on its own? He'd never needed anything so desperately or strained so wildly to get anything as he had to take a single breath of air. But, for an eternity, he couldn't get any at all. Not a thimbleful.

Suddenly he thought of his pistol, and his stomach seemed to drop out of him. Where the hell was his pistol? "Esco, you nitwit, you asshole, go get my gun!" he said in a hoarse whisper.

Esco was standing in a slight crouch, gazing up as though in fear and awe of Sally Ann's threats raining down. He turned, poking his forefinger toward the floor of the tree house.

"Get my fuckin pistol!" Jerry commanded.

Looking betrayed and wounded, Esco began to creep out from under the floor and into the open as though he thought, if only he moved slowly enough, no one would notice him.

Weak and trembling, Jerry watched him, some part of him perverse enough to hope Esco might be shot to pieces. At least then his own disaster would be minor by comparison. At least then it would be possible to believe that a little justice was returning to a fickle world.

# 17

"Why don't you put on some clothes?" Toots said. He gathered up jeans, panties, sneakers, and a T-shirt and held them out to her while—her face shining with tears and her eyes wild and uncomprehending—she looked at him as though he'd lost his mind; but he nodded toward the cave and urged the clothes upon her with such patient authority that, oddly docile, or dumbfounded, she took them from him and did what he said.

He was not calm exactly; it was just that extreme circumstances often brought about in him a kind of strange indirection. He'd gone through Korea in exactly that frame of mind; as though such madness could not be countenanced, couldn't even be looked at too closely, as one did not look directly at a welder's arc or at the sun. Even when he was a child and his mother had sent him away, he had behaved just so: consenting to the unaccustomed barbershop haircut with its cold, hard clippers and sweet-smelling tonic; consenting to the tag around his neck with his name and destination on it; the parting hug; and finally, to the disappearance of everything familiar beyond the bus's window. And many times during his long marriage he had survived by just such autistic indirection; at least until that morning when, for some reason or other, he had awakened.

He sat down to put on his black high-top tennis shoes and one of his old blue T-shirts that had faded toward a peculiar purple, while, once again, the world took one of its singular turns. Of course he had known he was tempting fate, one way or another, when he'd first provoked her to talk to him, never mind when he'd draped her over his shoulder like a haversack and carried her up into the tree house. And if he hadn't expected his present circumstances, he'd feared something equally bizarre. Yet when she was out of the cave and beside him before he'd even quite pulled his T-shirt over his head, he couldn't be sorry.

"Well," he said, "I wonder what they're up to?" But just as he spoke, the floor began to make small snapping noises here and there; little splinters of it seemed to jump up in the air; the galvanized tub made a metallic sound as though someone had flicked it with a fingernail; one of Sally Ann's new blouses hopped off the chair where she'd put it; and Toots got a sudden terrific pain in the ball of his left foot. "Shitfire," he said and dragged Sally Ann back in the cave with him, where he sat down on the bunk and took his basketball shoe off again. "They're shooting through the floor," he said.

Except that it was much more sudden and violent, the pain was halfway between stepping on a bee and stepping on a nail. Having gone through the floor and the sole of his shoe, the bullet seemed to be no more than half an inch into the fleshy pad of his foot, but he wanted it out. Even the smallest blade of his pocket knife was a little too wide, but he gripped his foot with all the strength his left hand could muster and dug away at the wound, which, curiously, hardly bled; at least until he'd dug out the mauled little piece of copper-coated lead, then it bled a lot, but it also felt much better. Sally Ann had watched with the heels of her hands pressed against her jaw and her fingertips clamped between her teeth. "Billy Wayne, you asshole!" she screamed suddenly, her eyes round and swimming with tears. "Who the hell do you think you are?"

"Billy Wayne couldn't come," Jerry replied from beneath the floor. "He sent us instead."

"You nasty little weasel!" Sally Ann shouted, "what do you want?"

"If you think about it a little, I bet you'll guess," came the response.

Looking at Toots and wiping tears with both hands, Sally Ann said, "You don't fool me, not for a minute! You mean to kill us and I know it!"

The pain in his foot had subsided enough so that he no longer had to squeeze it, and since he had no bandage, he thought it would offer some protection to put his shoe on again; the hole in the rubber bottom had all but closed and the sole seemed nearly as good as new.

"Now, now," Jerry said, "don't get crazy. We just want the money back; we're not interested in hurting anybody."

"I'll burn it!" Sally Ann said. "You shoot anymore, and I'll burn it! You know I'll do it, you nasty little shit!" she said, and before Toots could stop her, she was out of the cave and had her laundry bag full of money.

Toots hobbled out behind her, the inside of his left shoe growing slick and sticky at once. "Come on, come on," he said and tried to haul her back into the cave, but she pulled away.

"I'm gonna give them a demonstration," she said and, looking wildly about, snatched up one of Toots' pots and spied the demijohn under the sideboard where he kept kerosene for the lamps. A double handful of Billy Wayne Roland's money, two or three generous dashes of kerosene, and she struck a match.

"This is what shooting off your little gun costs!" she shouted, opening the screen door and dashing eight or ten flaming bundles of twenty-dollar bills into the darkness. "You do the least little thing I don't like, and I'll burn all of it!" she shouted. "You hear me, you assholes? You hear me?"

But they did not answer. Instead there was a lot of scurrying about and a lot of pounding and stamping and confusion and cursing: "There, there! Let me get . . . Beat it out! That crazy bitch! Over there! Jesus! Get that one! Maybe the water would . . . Ouch! Goddamn her. And that one too! For Christ's sake get it out! Goddamn!" they said.

Sally Ann gathered up her sack of money and ducked

under his arm to take some of his weight. "How can you walk?" she said. "Is it hurting awful?"

He shook his head, more in awe of her than in answer to her question, while she steered him back to the cave and plunked him down on his bunk. In fact, although he'd heard that being shot through the hand or foot was the most painful sort of wound, his foot hurt very little; perhaps because the wound was shallow, in the fleshy part of his foot, and hadn't reached any of the tiny bones or complicated sinew.

"That ought to give the bastards something to think about," she said.

"Would you really burn it all?" he asked.

"Every dollar," she said.

"Maybe if you just gave it to them, they'd leave, like they said."

If she had been capable of regret, she would have been very sorry to have gotten Toots into such trouble; but it was horrible to imagine being alone, even if there was nothing he could do to protect her. They wouldn't go away if she gave them the money; she knew they wouldn't. She knew the man who had sent them too well to believe he only wanted his money. She knew him better than his mother. Better than God. Her very fear, which had run like electricity through her body, which had struck at her heart and the marrow of her bones, was sufficient, by itself, to teach her what they would do. The money was not all they wanted. Maybe it was only the excuse; she couldn't be sure. She was only sure that killing her was the worst she would allow them to do. She had drawn a line; and, one way or another, she'd see that no one crossed it.

If she had answered Toots, she didn't remember it. She'd been looking at him with what would have been regret if only she had not been so grateful for him; but he seemed to think he'd been answered, for he nodded solemnly and said, "Well, I guess if we can hold out till morning, a fisherman might come by."

"The money's the only thing I've got to hurt them with," she said, and her chin went weak and tremulous for a moment before she straightened it out. "I don't think they would have come for me if I hadn't taken it, but they won't leave if I give it to them. It's the only weapon we've got."

He nodded again. "We'll just have to outlast them," he said, but he found himself looking at his chimney, or the narrow fissure in the ceiling that had served him as a chimney ever since he'd first built a fire in the cave. The far side of it was black where the smoke seemed literally to crawl up the wall, around a bulge and into the devious and ragged crack. He got up and hobbled over for a closer look while the man called Jerry began to harangue them again from somewhere underneath the floor of the tree house.

"That was a real cute trick," he said, "burning up the only thing that'll save your silly ass. What do you think? You think we're gonna go back and tell Mr. Roland that we asked nicely but you just wouldn't give his money back? Huh?"

The crevice above the firepit was narrow, though fairly long. Toots stuck his head through the opening and looked up, but it was dark as the inside of a cow and he couldn't see anything. He worked at it until he had forced his shoulders and the upper part of his chest inside the fissure and could reach up to find what might be there. The sweet stench of old fires filled his nostrils, but his hands found unexpected pockets of space as well as sharp and unyielding projections and outcroppings of rock. He could still hear Jerry's voice, if not precisely what he was saying, since the fissure itself seemed to be making some long, soft, breathy noise like a conch shell. He wiggled out again, scraping his shoulder and the tip of his ear.

"What is it?" Sally Ann said. "Can we get out through there?"

He shook his head. "I don't think so," he said, "but it might make a hell of a place to hide. I just don't know how much room there is."

"So what will it be?" Jerry called. "You can throw down

Mr. Roland's money and tell us good-bye; or you can make us get nasty. It's your choice."

Her lips trembling, she looked about as though in one last, distracted attempt to spot some alternative, but she made no sounds of weeping. "Can we get in there?"

Toots shrugged. "I'll see," he said.

"Are you gonna be smart or what?" Jerry called.

"Fuck off!" Sally Ann shouted. "I told you what I'd do!"

The second time, he managed to get his head and chest inside the opening with a bit less trouble, but it was hard to find a way to brace himself in order to draw the rest of his body up into the fissure. Still, at last, he managed to do it only to crack his head on the sharp point of a rock. He felt surrounded on all sides so that it seemed impossible to move any part of his body, but finally he was able to twist to one side, and with a rock digging into his kidney and another scraping his chest, he raised himself a few feet into the devious fissure. Then, to his surprise, he found he was able to worm into another part of the chimney, and by bracing himself with his hands and knees, he managed to climb upward for a distance, although he couldn't be sure how far. He was even beginning to hope that, by some miracle, they might find a clever escape when he came to a spot so crooked and narrow he couldn't get past it. He struggled and contorted himself until, horribly, he got wedged with his left arm somehow folded against his chest and his head twisted to one side so that he seemed to be breathing the detritus of crumbling rock into his nostrils. He fought hard against panic while the narrow chimney seemed to press in on him from all sides as though to smother him. Finally he found some purchase with his toes, and in desperation, shoved himself upward as hard as he could. He tried to pull his left arm down, but felt instead the wall of the chimney make a little grating shift against his forearm and felt, as well, the cool breath of outside air. He had thought he was facing inward toward the bluff but realized that somehow he had gotten turned the other way. Just the touch of outside air against his arm was enough to allow the worst of his panic to retreat; he realized he could breathe after all, even if he was firmly caught. He knew, as well, that it would be bad to allow anything to fall down the outside of the bluff, and so, give himself away. Carefully, slowly, he was able to get the fingers of his right hand up under his left elbow to claw and work at the rotten rock, so that whatever small amount of it he could loosen and pull away would fall back down the inside of the chimney. Finally he was able to dig free a rock a little smaller than a brick, and then a larger one. He stopped the smaller one with his leg and pressed it against the side of the chimney with his thigh to keep it from falling, but the larger one got away and bounced down the inside of the chimney below him. He could only hope the men outside did not hear it. Still, he managed to free his left arm; and, when he slid back down the chimney a little way, he could see starshine through a small hole in the bluff. For a while he rested and looked out while his heartbeat slowed. He couldn't see the floodplain below, but he could mark the tops of trees against the horizon across the river. He could have put his arm out in space to the elbow, but he did not. Instead he felt gently around the opening to see how it was composed. He thought he could make it bigger, but he didn't know if he could make it big enough to crawl through, and he didn't know how long it might take him even if he could. He knew it would help to have something to work with—a screwdriver, or better, a claw hammer. But it would be foolish for them to emerge on the face of the bluff with those men below, particularly since he didn't know how far he was from the top. Over the years, when it was extremely cold, he had always retreated to the cave and tended a fire there; and often, during his comings and goings, he'd noticed smoke issuing from half a dozen different spots along the ragged face of the bluff, but he had no notion which of those vents he might have discovered. Perhaps he'd even made a new one. But, now that he'd cleared the way a bit, he thought he'd try climbing a little higher. The rock seemed to get more rotten and full of fractures the farther up he went—maybe the insinuating pressure of roots from the scrub that grew on top, or the rain, or the freezings and thawings of winter—he couldn't say just why.

# 18

Jerry sent Esco down to the river to soak the hemp sacks they had found under the tree house, and while Esco was gone, he continued to threaten Sally Ann in order to keep her occupied. Although his spine still felt limp and he was shaky from his fall, he was so cheered that, when Esco returned, he laughed, slapped him on the back, and even pinched his round cheeks, as coarse with stubble as a wire brush. He could see that such behavior confused Esco more than it pleased him, since he was naturally accustomed to abuse, but it didn't matter. Of the ten thousand dollars she had set afire, only a few hundred had actually burned, a little more was scorched around the edges, and the rest merely smelled of coal oil. Hell, he had them. He knew he did. Before the sun rose again he'd be independent, a new man entirely, who would never again consent to take orders from anyone.

Even Esco had been made to understand that, if they'd had anything to fight with, they wouldn't be burning money. Even Esco, if you laid it all out for him and waited a while for the fog to lift, could be made to see the obvious. Still he thought it best to explain to him what he should do one more time.

If Esco could get off the roof and inside before she could set the money afire, so much the better, but if not, he was to throw it down at once so it could be smothered out with the wet sacks. "Then, if you want, you can throw down that one-eyed old fart and that silly bitch too." Jerry couldn't resist pinching Esco's cheek again and laughing, but Esco wiped the offending hand away as though he suspected

Jerry might be developing a new and confusing way to abuse him—no one, since he'd moved away from his mother, had pinched his cheeks, and he didn't understand what to make of it or quite what to do about it. Somehow it both gave him a small, deep thrill and angered him.

# 19

At first Sally Ann had been able to hear him scuffling and scratching about inside the fissure like a mouse behind a wall—at least that's the way he would have sounded if it weren't for his labored breathing and harsh grunts and groans—but she couldn't hear him any longer. She had crouched beside the opening and waited while soft black soot or occasional puffs of feathery ashes sifted down; but now, if anything fell, it was coarse sand and small, sharp shards of rock. She wished the hell he'd climb back down. He had been gone forever, and she thought he must have climbed a great way off. She wrung her hands, so frightened her stomach fluttered as though it were a bird beating its wings against a window.

"Saallee, ooohh Saaallleee," Jerry called in a new sing-songy voice, "you better throw that fuckin money down, or you'll wish like hell you had."

Something heavy was falling inside the chimney; she could hear it hitting. It seemed to come from high up, and it caused a shower of grit and coarse sand to rain from the opening. But then, whatever it was hit somewhere and quit falling. "Toots?" she whispered into the crevice, "Toots?"

"Let me put it another way," Jerry called. "You busted Billy Wayne's head. Right? You mangled his goddamned dick, you swiped his fuckin car and stole a quarter of a million goddamned dollars from him! Now you probably just don't realize how depressed he is about all that. Right? I mean he's just not sweet on you anymore. You understand? Hey, if he were here, he'd have pieces of your cute little ass spread all over the woods by now. You're lucky it's only me and Esco. Hell, it's nothing personal with us. We just want the money back. So why don't you just go on and toss it down while we're still in a good mood."

She didn't know where Toots had gotten to, but she decided she'd rather be with him than alone. "Toots?" she said into the crevice, "Toots, I'm coming up." She was answered by the dull clatter of rocks falling down the inside of the fissure. She seemed to hear a lot of them, but only one actually rattled out of the opening and fell into the firepit. She didn't want to be conked on the head, but she wanted, even less, to be by herself, listening to Jerry. For almost a minute after the rock fell, a steady stream of sand and grit rained from the crevice, but when it stopped, she leaned into the opening and whispered fiercely, "Toots, come back!"

What if he was stuck up there, she thought? What if she tried to follow and somehow couldn't even find him? She could feel her mouth twist itself toward weeping, and for a moment she cried until the painful knot at the base of her throat seemed to loosen and dissolve; then, as though the crying were merely an irritating little chore she'd had to get out of the way, she took her laundry bag and went out into the tree house, where she gathered up the new clothes Toots had bought her and stuffed them in the bag on top of the money and then stuffed Toots' new clothes on top of hers.

"Goddamn it, you're not the only one who can light a fire, you know," Jerry called. "We could burn you out any time. What the hell, we got nothing to lose. Right? You better smarten up. We're not going to wait around down here all night!"

"Good! Be sure and leave your address, so I'll know where to write," she shouted, her voice still full of the fractured notes and uneven scales of weeping.

She was back in the cave before she grew unsure. Perhaps she should wait a little longer. As frightening as it was to be alone, it would be worse yet to leave the tree house undefended when the two of them might have to come back to it only to find Jerry and Esco smug and waiting. But all at once her heart jumped with happiness and she leaned toward the crevice to listen, certain she heard Toots' soft scuffling again. She did, she was sure she did. And she heard loose debris falling as well, but, strangely, the sound didn't seem to be coming from the opening above the firepit, although it seemed to be above her. Just as she realized dirt and rock had begun to fall on the roof of the tree house, she heard a great commotion coming down the chimney as well. Still, she didn't have a chance to be confused, since, in the next moment, something hit the roof of the tree house like a bomb. It cracked wood, rattled windows, and caused something somewhere to fall from a shelf. Rushing out of the cave, she was stunned by the sight of a leg sticking through the ceiling. It was a naked leg whose trousers had been unable to follow it through the hole it had made, a hairy leg that had been scraped raw in a spot or two, a very thick leg with a nylon sock and a black street shoe on it, and it did not belong to Toots. She knew who it belonged to, and when it started trying to withdraw, she decided, instantly, not to let it. She was across the room, on a chair, and had it by the ankle before it had risen six inches.

"Hey," its owner said, "cut it out," and the leg began to pull back, taking her with it. Her feet left the chair, but she hung on. "Cut it out," Esco said again, pulling her up until her head nearly touched the ceiling before he seemed to tire and she found herself sinking once again toward the chair. "Let go. You let go now!" Esco said, and she found herself rising a second time with a great deal more force and power, but then Toots, as filthy as a gutter rat, was beside her, looping coils of rope around Esco's ankle and securing them with quick, artful hitches. Before she quite knew what had happened, Toots had the other end of the rope around a leg of the cast-iron cook stove and had taken such a strain, the cook stove actually moved an inch or two across the floor. Quick as a cowboy hogtying a steer, Toots whipped up a knot. "Hey, cut that out now!" Esco cried while the roof groaned ominously, and the stove grated across the floor enough to put a gentle bend in the stovepipe.

"Mercy," Toots said and gave the ceiling a brief, doubtful glance, his eye rolling white in his grimy face, "come on before he breaks through."

Since he knew the way, he went first, reaching down a hand to pull her up when he could, waiting and whispering instructions when the chimney was too narrow or crooked to offer her any help. But she was just small enough to manage very well, and since he was pushing the laundry bag ahead of him, it wasn't long until she seemed to be constantly on his heels, almost, in fact, clawing at them. They tried to be as quiet as they could, but Esco was making such a racket, it didn't seem to matter—Toots was certain he'd heard the stovepipe fall before he'd even quite hoisted Sally Ann out of the cave, and since then, Esco had been more or less bellowing like a bull.

At last Toots came to the place where a part of the fissure took a right-angle turn and he could look out into the treetops. The opening seemed clearly large enough to crawl through, although it was hidden from any but the most direct line of sight by an overhanging rock. He had been just there and looking out when Esco's huge, unlikely bulk had passed down the bluff directly in front of him. There had been a moment when he and Esco had been eye to eye and only three feet apart, although he could see very little of Esco by starshine; and, no doubt, Esco could see nothing at all of him, tucked away, as he was, like an animal in the pitch-black weem of its den. Toots had started back down the chimney at once, but going backward was slower than climbing. He got stuck more often; at least until, in desperation, he let himself go limp and tried to fall out of the chimney. He got down much faster after that, although he took some hard knocks and scrapes.

"What is it?" Sally Ann whispered behind him, "what's the matter?"

"Shhh," he told her, and pushing the laundry sack cautiously ahead of him, he eased himself out of the opening.

He craned his neck to look down, but the bluff bellied out below him, and he could only see the far edge of his roof, polished faintly silver in the moonlight. Esco had quit begging and bellowing, but Toots could hear his great, drawn-out, straining grunts as he tried to draw the heavy cook stove across the floor, or maybe, God forbid, lift it through the roof.

"This don't change nothing," Jerry insisted from somewhere down on the floodplain. "Hey, this don't change a goddamned thing. I'm the one you gotta deal with, and the more you piss me off, the worse it's gonna be."

He helped Sally Ann crawl out behind him, and they crept over the top of the bluff and hurried away, his wounded foot growing sticky and sore inside his shoe as Sally Ann plunged ahead, pulling him along behind her as though he were a reluctant child. Once in a while he reined her in just long enough to point out the direction they should take, but then she'd be off again, gripping his hand and straining ahead while her breath came in squeaks and sobs. "Whoa," he said when they broke into a small clearing where the juniper and broom straw seemed frosted over with moonlight. "Whoa now." He set his heels and pulled her up short, although in the next moment she managed to drag him another step or two.

"No!" she said. "Come on! Come on!"

"Shhh," he told her, "we're clear now. There's no need to run ourselves to death. Shhh," he said, struggling with her, trying to calm and contain her, petting her as though she were some wild creature he meant to gentle with his touch. "They don't know we've gotten away. They think they've still got us." She trembled and shook, but at last she began to nod while the squeaks and sobs drained out of her breathing. "We're fine," he told her. Perhaps he was simply too old to be as frightened as she was. Perhaps he had merely been too surprised. He didn't know. More than anything he felt giddy, but that was a complicated emotion, he suspected, no more than one part happiness. Still, he half wanted to dance a jig or laugh out loud as if he'd played a marvelous prank on someone. If not on the fellows he'd left back at his camp, then maybe on his own dull, singular fate. For who could have imagined that someone like Sally Ann would appear to yank him out of his rut and drag him away through the moonlight?

# 20

By the time Esco took his first exhausted and despairing rest against the roof, the shank of his leg already scrubbed raw by the rough hemp rope, Toots and Sally Ann had broken out of the scrub oak and juniper, slipped past the ritzy colony of standoffish houses, and started down the Cove Creek Pike toward Clifton. By the time Jerry got the dark suspicion that, somehow, impossibly, he might be threatening an empty house, they were washing themselves in a farmer's stock pond on the outskirts of town, the huge mottled shapes of Holsteins around them, blowing softly through their nostrils and staring with bovine curiosity as the two of them broke the surface of the watering hole, left soiled pieces of their clothing on the trodden earth, dressed once more, climbed the fence, and went on down the moon-drenched road.

Later, at the bus station, surrounded by the stench of urine and institutional soap, they washed again, bought two collapsible red plaid suitcases and two tickets on the first bus out of town, which happened to be going to Memphis. They were boarding before Jerry dared test his suspicion that, except for the infuriating idiot on the roof, he was alone. He stood off at a distance of forty feet and emptied his pistol randomly into the side of the tree house. Nothing. He reloaded, emptied again, and got a whining ricochet off the stove. "Don't," Esco pleaded from the roof, "that's dangerous!"

"Shut up, you dumb fuck," Jerry said. Maybe they were merely trying to bring him within range of some nasty trick. Perhaps they meant to make him think that, somehow, magically, they had gotten away when, in fact, they were waiting to ambush him. But why hadn't they turned out their lights before they started to play possum? It didn't make sense. What outraged him was that nothing about them had ever made any sense. It was enough to make him froth at the mouth. He loaded his pistol again, found a likely tree on the far side of the garden, and with a great deal of effort, managed, at last, to climb even a bit higher than the catwalk. He couldn't see all of the room, but he could see the rope from Esco's ankle to the stove, and while he watched, one corner of the stove lifted three or four inches off the floor and then thumped back again, making the single noise he'd been hearing for the better part of an hour. Esco was hopeless. A dumb animal beating its head against the wall. An idiot. A pitiful, subhuman fuckup. He had a strong desire to shoot Esco between the eyes, but he reminded himself that the only thing worth his attention was the money. His money, since Billy Wayne would never see a nickel of it. With a quarter of a million dollars in his pocket, he'd never have to suffer fools again, at least not the sort of fool who was also his boss. That money belonged to him. He'd paid for it in aggravation, and he was not about to let some simple bitch off the street bluff him out of it. If he did, then he might as well cut his own throat and have done with it. He climbed down out of the tree, trembling but determined. After a quarter of an hour of luckless searching for what he needed, he had to settle for the aluminum boat, which was noisy and clumsy and heavy to boot, although not nearly as heavy as the others.

A little at a time, he was able to drag it from the water to the base of the bluff. It was a great struggle to stand it on its stern and prop its bow on the sheer face of the cliff—one slip and he'd sound like a bunch of Virgin Island blacks playing in a steel band. He did the best he could, but he wasn't able to help a small metallic boom or two, and he waited a full fifteen minutes after he got the boat in place before he began to climb quietly from seat to seat, and finally to the prow. Balancing on that, he was able to reach the catwalk and pull himself up. He took care to stay low enough so that Esco couldn't look over the eaves and see him. He knew Esco was too stupid to keep quiet if he caught sight of him. "Hey, Jerry!" he'd bellow, "make em untie my foot and let me go!"

Scarcely breathing, moving only inches at a time, he eased around the catwalk until he came to the edge of a window. He took the oblique view it offered of the far end of the room. Nothing. No one. Not a sign of life. He slid under the window like a shadow and scanned the near end of the room from the other side. Crude shelves and a curtain half-covering what appeared to be the entrance to a cave. That had to be it then; they were somewhere in the cave. He thought a moment, the pistol cocked and ready against his chest, his back to the wall: they had to be somewhere in the cave because no one would set ten thousand dollars on fire if they could simply get away. He crept to the screen door and inspected as much of the room as he could from the edge of it. Esco raised one corner of the stove and let it thump back against the floor, and even though he'd heard Esco gathering effort on the roof, a stubborn sound which was neither quite grunt nor sob, and even though he'd seen one leg of the stove rise up, the sudden thump caused his heart to race, and he cowered beside the door for a moment before he made another move. At last, when he had gotten himself under control and had convinced himself that there was no one in the tree house, he pushed gently on the screen door, but the spring at the top strummed and popped, and he paused to unhook it before he tried again.

Scarcely fifteen miles away the diesel engine was changing pitch and the brakes were moaning and hissing as the bus pulled up nonchalantly in front of what appeared to be more drugstore than bus stop. The driver opened the doors for a very fat black woman carrying a shopping bag who seemed to take forever to hoist herself up the steps. Sally Ann had to grip the armrest to keep from shouting at her to hurry up, but the woman took her own good time getting aboard and then probing around in her purse to find her money, which she handed over a single bill and coin at a time. When she'd been given her ticket, she seemed to have to tuck all sorts of things away in their proper places before she could gather up her parcels and come down the aisle, listing heavily from side to side like a ship in a storm. Even then the bus driver didn't make any effort to drive on but began to dicker with papers on a clipboard. Sally Ann searched the street and sidewalk, half-expecting to see Jerry's smug face appear to stare knowingly at her through the window. She closed her eyes in order to shut out the possibility, but opened them with a terrible start when she heard a banging at the side of the bus. The driver had opened the luggage compartment and lifted out a large cardboard carton, which he carried into the drugstore and delivered. She watched him chat amiably with a woman behind the cash register. Finally he came out and climbed aboard again, and she closed her eyes once more until the doors clattered shut, and with a huge pneumatic sigh, the bus began to grind ahead.

She simply could not calm herself. On the one hand she was endlessly surprised that no one seemed to be taking any particular notice of her or Toots, and on the other she knew she was perilously close to attracting all sorts of attention. At any moment she might plead with the driver to go faster or beg him to pass up his scheduled stops. At any moment she might begin to babble to everyone on the bus in an effort to explain away her discolored eye and puffy lip; the cheap, suspiciously new suitcases shoved under their seats; or the dark red stain soaking upward from the sole of one of Toots' sporty new shoes. A car overtook them and blinked its lights to pass, and she grabbed Toots' hand and squeezed until she saw that it was not a car at all but a pickup.

"When did they say we'd get to Memphis?" she whispered fiercely. "I can't remember."

"One forty-five," Toots told her.

"Not if he stops at every little crossroads," she said in a voice full of squeaks.

"It doesn't matter," he said softly. "They won't find you now."

"Ha," she said, "you've told me that before."

But at one forty-five they were rolling down the wide, well-lit avenues of Memphis, and no one was in pursuit, since, even then, Esco was lying on their roof like a great, lumpish bundle of wet wash, and Jerry was sitting at their dinner table.

Jerry had discovered right away that they had climbed up through the ragged crack in the roof of the cave, but he'd been too smart to try and crawl in after them, since if they were hiding, that could be exactly what they wanted. Instead he'd made threats and struck bargains for half an hour before he set a blanket afire and stuffed it in the fissure with a broom handle. All the while Esco had bellowed and begged to be turned loose, but Jerry paid no attention. Somehow he could no longer bear to think of Esco as his partner, and his hatred of him had grown as unreasonable as it was powerful. Esco had had his chance, and now when those two were caught, he, Jerry, would do the catching while that worthless son of a bitch suffered his proper, ridiculous fate.

But a few minutes after the thick, acrid smoke from the blanket began to fill the crevice, and there was no begging, no desperate ruckus from inside it, an empty feeling began to creep around in Jerry's stomach. He went out on the catwalk and watched the smoke rise against the stars from half a dozen vents along the top of the bluff. But he paused only an instant before, with despairing, frantic haste, he let down the ladder and snatched a lantern from the tree house. While Esco pleaded from the roof, he made the long circling climb to the top of the bluff where he found, at last, exactly what he feared he would find: proof positive that Sally Ann had played him for a fool. The moment he found the spot where they had crawled out and where the stench of the blanket he had burned still lingered, he fell to his knees. As though nothing could be more surprising than discovering just what he'd expected, each nerve in his body felt singed with sudden electricity, his hands shook violently, and his vision turned inward and blank.

It was a very long time before anything like reasonable thought returned and he could speculate about how long they might have been gone. Hours probably. He knew he'd never be able to track them in the dark. He no longer had the spirit to try. It was all he could do to get to his feet. He fumbled with the ungainly pistol until he got it tucked inside his belt and, like a man walking in his sleep, climbed back down to the tree house where he slumped into a chair by the table.

He sat there still, trying to imagine what sort of abuse he'd have to take from Billy Wayne when the circumstances of this night came out. It was possible that not only Billy Wayne but Esco might be his boss in the future, and almost dispassionately he realized he deserved no better treatment. There was little sense in trying to fool himself about it. He'd called up all the courage he could muster against a one-eyed old fool and a silly little bitch who'd had nothing, literally nothing, to defend themselves with, and still he'd managed to cower and skulk about until they'd gotten away. As ill as it made him feel to admit it, on some level or other he knew he was better off. If he'd been able to get his hands on Billy Wayne's quarter of a million, he'd still have the illusion he was some sort of gangster, and sooner or later the real item would have shown up and eaten him for breakfast.

But it was such a pitiful waste of talent. All his life he'd felt a secret hoard of wickedness in him, which was like being more powerful than other people—having more options, having the edge. But he could see now that he'd only had the illusion of power. He'd only thought himself sinister and lawless. Perhaps because he loved himself so much, he was also a coward and couldn't bear putting himself in hazardous situations; therefore his delicious sense of wickedness was sterile and useless. It made him feel washed out and weak to acknowledge it, but it seemed utterly inescapable. It was as though he'd been born with a tail and thought he could swing from the trees with it. But the essential truth was, he was simply in the wrong line of work.

For some moments, as though in a daze, he considered Esco's burly leg thrust through the ceiling, the fallen stovepipe, the stove itself, dragged half off its protective sheet of tin. Esco, he suspected, had finally passed out. Perhaps he'd broken something or hurt himself when he'd fallen. Perhaps he'd only gotten tired and decided to take a little nap. Whatever, he didn't have the stomach to hear any more bellowing or any threats, and as quietly as he could, he rose, opened the screen door, and crept down the ladder.

It took a little while to get the outboard engine to run, but finally it sputtered and fired, and he started back down the river in the moonlight. Just as he feared, when he came abreast of the tree house, he saw the hulking shape on the roof lift itself up like some awful behemoth to watch him pass. "Jerry, you come back here!" it bawled. "You come back here right now!" But he gripped the throttle and kept his steady course, and after he'd gone a mile or so, he began to take some sort of minimal stock of himself. His skin was still more or less in one piece. Scorched and smelling of kerosene though it was, he had somewhere between eight and ten thousand dollars. And finally, he had the absolute knowledge that he was a coward. The admission made little needles of pain pierce his stomach as though he'd swallowed a pincushion, and it seemed to drain all the strength out of his limbs, but it had one virtue he could appreciate: cowardice was, after all, an irreducible endowment from which nothing, absolutely nothing, could be taken away, and there was no reason why he couldn't build a life on it.

When the lights of Clifton began to appear along the shore and he throttled the engine down, he discovered a sweaty key in his palm where apparently it had been since he'd unlocked the boat. Without a second thought he pitched it over his shoulder. But the pistol, jammed painfully against his belly, was another matter. He drew it, wondering if its blued, heavy potency could still inspire him, but merely the act of weighing it in his hand filled him with desolation. He couldn't quite watch himself do it, but he hung the pistol over the side of the boat and let it slip, as though by accident, into the dark water.

When he saw the soft shine of moonlight on the chrome of Esco's car, he felt a little better. All his old obligations were gone, it seemed to him, just as completely as if he'd committed suicide. All he had to do was hot-wire the Camaro, drive to Nashville, pick up his own car and his clothes, and take himself far away. To California, say. Never again would he have anything to do with people who were vulgar and dangerous. He'd cultivate charm and good manners. He'd dress with exquisite taste and style. And he'd find something to do that suited him. He'd sell something. Real estate, say.

As he was nudging the boat into shore, far up the river Esco lay face down on the roof, rolling the heavy ridge of his brow back and forth against the gritty surface of the tar paper, occupied with gathering strength and making an old and familiar pact with betrayal. When he was younger he'd had to make his secret, terrible peace with betrayal every day. He knew how it was done. You merely had to turn everything into its opposite so that pain became a grim sort of pleasure and an insult became just another sort of greeting that provided you with a challenge. You kept strict account, and when you could, you dealt out pain and humiliation to balance the books. Otherwise being constantly tricked and taunted by those who were brighter and quicker would break you down. Only he'd thought he'd left all that behind. He'd thought it belonged to his childhood, his school days, and he'd got beyond it.

He knew better now, and he rolled his heavy brow back and forth on the roof while he denied the ring of fire around his ankle and the feeling in his hip that his leg had been all but pulled from its socket. He concentrated until he was able to convert the hot pain around the shank of his leg into his own positive grip on the rope and until the strained feeling in his hip became little more than the impatience of great strength. After some time, when the conversion was complete, he gathered himself and began to lift with all his might until the roof groaned and the rope strummed. He meant to make the roof collapse or cause the rope to break, but neither of those things happened. Instead, with a terrific iron boom and clatter that shook the whole building, he merely toppled the stove over on its back. Still, the knot tied around the leg of the stove was suddenly three feet off the floor, and he was able to withdraw his foot and untie himself, impressed but not at all surprised with what he could do when he remembered again just who he was.

# 21

From Memphis they took an express to Little Rock because Sally Ann thought no one would ever expect them to go to Arkansas—she certainly had never thought of going there—but once they got to Little Rock, she thought she'd feel safer if they made one more unlikely jump before they settled, and they took a plane to St. Louis. Someone they had ridden with from Clifton to Memphis just might have seen them board the bus to Little Rock. How Billy Wayne would find such a person, she didn't know, but the idea made her nervous. Besides, Little Rock was a bit small, she thought, and she and Toots, being strangers, might attract too much attention. St. Louis was a better idea; it was another place no one would think of, and it was bigger.

When they got to St. Louis, Toots went straight to a hospital emergency room and got a tetanus shot and some antibiotics for his foot, which had grown feverish and sore. He'd stepped on a nail, he told them.

They rented a motel room and a post office box; and, while they tried to gather around them at least the appearance of normalcy, Sally Ann wrote for duplicates of her social security card, her driver's license, her credit cards, and any other form of identification that might, from time to time, pop into her mind. She had her hair cut short and dyed coppery brown. She wore a large pair of rose-colored glasses wherever she went. But she slept poorly and refused to spend more than two nights at the same lodging. She bought traveler's checks of various kinds from various banks. She bought government savings bonds at the post office. She bought clothes and luggage. But she remained fearful and nervous. More than that, she seemed beset by some deeper discontent, and sometimes she would grow so tearful and snappish, Toots felt he must somehow be to blame and would half make up his mind to tell her good-bye. But then her mood would change abruptly, and she would fall into his arms and tell him he was the nicest, sweetest man in all the world, and she didn't know what would become of her without him. The trouble was, except in moments of love-making, she seemed distant and out of reach; and, with him or without him, he didn't know what was going to become of her. Or him.

After almost a month of eating a great deal of Chinese and Italian food, seeing dozens of movies, and spending long hours beside the swimming pools of various motels, Sally Ann saw a man she knew in the dining room of the Holiday Inn where they were staying. She remembered him clearly because he had left her especially large tips when she was a cocktail waitress at Billy Wayne's club. She even remembered his name, which was Loomis something, or something Loomis. It did no good for Toots to insist the man couldn't possibly have recognized her, since he himself scarcely recognized her anymore. "Ha," she said, "but what about you! Look at yourself, for Christ's sake! You've got one eye and only half a nose!"

It didn't do any good either to argue that he'd never met this Loomis fellow at all. She was convinced that sooner or later the man would be back in Billy Wayne's club and sooner or later the subject of Sally Ann and her one-eyed cohort would come up—hell, who was to say it hadn't come up already. It was perfectly possible that ten minutes after Loomis had left the dining room, he was putting in a call to Nashville. Anyway, she insisted, it was silly to stay in St. Louis any longer. If she could get most all of her identification back, if such remnants of her past life could come to her through the mail, then who was to say Billy Wayne might not show up. He was known to be friendly with the police and all sorts of important people. And hadn't Toots gone to the Veterans Administration and had his records transferred to St. Louis, and wasn't he receiving his benefits? It was plain to her they'd been pushing their luck for some time now. Anyway, she'd already picked out another place that Billy Wayne wouldn't think of in a thousand years.

So that very afternoon they took a flight to Minneapolis–St. Paul, and not much more than a week after they got there, Toots had a glass eye that, bedazzled and askew, might stare with what seemed insane fascination at the treetops, the hubcaps of passing cars, or the breasts of some flustered lady sitting across the aisle from him on a city bus. He even agreed to be fitted for a little lump of flesh-colored plastic to replace the missing bridge of his nose. And when he got it, there was no denying it fit between his eyes as neatly as the piece of a puzzle, although the color was never quite right and it did something to his voice that made him sound like a duck, or anyway, as though he had a perpetual head cold. Also, although it didn't hurt exactly, it did feel a little like a wedge driven into his face, and it pressed on some subterranean passage that bothered his breathing. As a consequence he only wore it when he went out, or when, much later in the fall, some of Sally Ann's friends came to visit.

They took a small unfurnished apartment just on the edge of one of St. Paul's many parks, and Sally Ann seemed almost happy; at least for as long as it took them to paint and paper, buy furniture, and settle in. But when all the work was done, she grew nervous and dissatisfied again. She decided she wanted to do something to improve herself and enrolled in two adult education courses taught in the evenings at a neighborhood high school. She wanted to take her GED test, get the equivalent of a high school diploma, and then, by God, go to college. But the homework vexed her, particularly the math, and although she asked for Toots' help, and he did his best, the homework sessions nearly always ended badly. More often than not, Toots couldn't work the problems himself, and even if he could, he couldn't seem to do them the way her teacher had. When he got the right answer using the wrong method, she might crumple her paper, throw her math book across the room, and stare at him furiously as though he had betrayed her. It was during such a moment—he had found the answer to one of her problems by some strange geometry of his own—that she first told him he sounded like a duck. It struck him as a very peculiar thing to say, not because it wasn't true, but because he didn't have his nose plug in at the time, and she'd said it out of the blue, as though it were a bone of contention between them, or as though they had been trading insults.

She stopped going to her adult education courses and bought a guitar, a book that was supposed to teach her to play it, and an African lovebird, which was green, blue, and black with white spots around its eyes and a very red beak. It looked like a miniature parrot and cost a great deal of money, and when Sally Ann wasn't perched before its cage trying to teach it to speak, she was holding the guitar in her lap, staring into the songbook and dragging her right thumb across the guitar strings as though they might have some vague itch. Toots told himself it was not a good thing for them to be together all day every day, and he took a job down at the docks on the Mississippi River. But he was beginning to know what he knew.

Finally Sally Ann began taking guitar lessons from a student at the University of Minnesota who had advertised his services in the paper. His name was Mark, and very soon he began to drop by one or two evenings a week for a drink. He was a dark-headed, handsome fellow who seemed to find nothing remarkable about Toots' and Sally Ann's living arrangements. But, then again, he gave the impression that nothing under the sun would surprise him. He was a philosophy student, an accomplished guitarist, a would-be playwright, an amateur hypnotist, and an expert in the martial arts. It took him no time at all to teach Sally Ann's bird to whistle like a wolf on a street corner and say, "Hot stuff!" With her guitar playing, however, he had less luck; but, after a while, how well she played the guitar no longer seemed very important. She had learned a number of chords, a bass run or two, and could accompany herself fairly well, at least on a few songs. Anyway, as she explained to Toots, there was no point in getting fantastically good because she could hardly afford to make a name for herself or become famous.

Through Mark she met a number of other university students and learned, to her astonishment, that she could take nearly any course she wanted through the university's Division of Continuing Education; and, unless she wanted a degree, the business of her high school diploma need never come up. She'd be just like any other college student, or almost. She was excited but very nervous over the prospect, and nothing Toots could think to say ever quite put her mind at ease. He'd never been to college, after all, and if she forgot that long enough to ask him what he thought, she remembered it before he said two words and hardly bothered to hide her impatience and disinterest. He couldn't very well blame her. If anyone was going to give her good advice about such things, it would have to be Mark and her new friends.

Soon she began to see so much of them that, more often than not, when Toots came home from work the apartment would be empty, and only the bird would be there to greet him, whistling, zipping from perch to perch in the fancy cage, and repeating its solitary remark over and over in its tiny, strangled voice. She seldom left a note and sometimes he fixed elaborate meals for them only to find himself obliged to eat alone when it grew very late and she did not appear. At such moments even the slight noise of a fork or knife against a plate, or perhaps the clink of a glass, seemed somehow significant, and he felt extraordinarily foolish as though he were just learning an emotion that every other member of his race had always recognized. It was such a vulnerable, desolate feeling, he didn't know how anyone could bear it. The best he could do was try to pretend it didn't exist, distract himself, train himself to take special note of all sorts of trivia—the silky sound that sugar made falling out of a spoon into a cup of coffee, the callus growing in the palm of his hand from the pushbroom he used in the warehouse, the number of bicycles he might see on the way to work—so that his spirit did not languish and despair when she was not around, or even, sometimes, when she was. He was surprised that he could divide himself against himself in such a fashion.

The second Friday in October she invited some of her friends to a small, informal party, and she was in a dither to get the apartment looking just so. She scattered pillows here and there, rearranged furniture to keep it from being quite so stiff and precise, snatched pictures off the wall as if they were obscene, and tacked up posters in their places—one of a canal in Venice, one of the Eiffel Tower, and another of a fellow playing a guitar who was wearing some sort of Buck Rogers costume and had painted his face like a savage. She threw a frilly, ribboned lamp shade she'd only recently bought in the trash, preferring a bare bulb to her former notions of beauty. And just when she seemed to have everything the way she wanted it, she rearranged it all again. When he had finished helping her with the nuts and cheeses and finger foods, she even decorated him, insisting he wear his eyepatch, arranging it and its elastic just so on his face and using her own makeup to blend in his nose plug until he thought his whole nose looked fake, although, it was true, the plug didn't show.

He didn't look forward to playing host, not with a nose that felt like a hood ornament and a voice that sounded like a duck, but her new friends were so casual and quickly at home, there was no need to offer them a drink or something to eat, or even show them where the bathroom was. They found whatever they required at once. There were four of them altogether: a young, rather delicate-looking poet they called Sheldon; a plump, sullen girl named Malissa, who wore a floppy hat and a serape and arrived already holding forth on the mistreatment of women and third world countries; a tall, dark, pretty girl named Deirdre, who was a print maker, wore blue jeans, a man's work shirt, and hiking boots, and who seldom spoke a word to anyone; and finally, Mark. Toots envied them their grace and confidence, the easy way they draped themselves comfortably on the furniture or floor, and amid the breathy sneezes of their beer cans opening, judged good and ill of art, politics, and men. It seemed to him they were even able to ignore his existence without being rude, as though they recognized at once that he, like Deirdre, had nothing he wished to say. In any case, Sheldon, Mark, and Malissa carried the burden of conversation quite happily. Even Sally Ann didn't have much to say, particularly since she, herself, soon became the principal topic of discussion. After that it seemed she could only listen with shining eyes and a rapt smile while first one and then another of her guests took turns at defining her personality and laying out her future. Obviously Sally Ann had the disposition of an artist, Mark declared, and he was certain that somewhere in the Fine Arts department she'd find her niche. And if you could throw a great pot or do a fine painting or make a print or act or weave or make jewelry, a degree was totally unnecessary and absolutely meaningless. Deirdre nodded while Malissa lit a joint, took a deep drag, and, after holding her breath until her eyes teared, assured everyone that Sally Ann could study any damned thing she chose, and if she did well, there were many ways around not having graduated from high school. That was a matter of no importance, Malissa insisted and passed the joint around; Sally Ann could become a lawyer or a goddamned federal judge if she wanted to. They all pondered that solemnly until Sheldon began to shake his small, fine head as though in awe. Sally Ann was so real, he said earnestly. They all waited for him to go on, but apparently that was the end of his contribution, although he repeated it throughout the evening with great emphasis and sincerity.

Toots sat on a kitchen stool just inside the door to the living room, a chest of beer at his feet and a bottle of bourbon at his elbow, and since no one else showed the slightest interest in the bourbon, he utilized it himself. Mute as a shadow against the wall, he watched Sally Ann trying hard to reinvent herself while he poured drink after drink from the fifth of Jim Beam until the bottle was two-thirds empty, and strangely, he had gone from a dizzy, bemused drunkenness to a painful lucidity. All at once it was clear to him that she simply didn't have any further use for him, and it would be foolish to pretend otherwise. There was no one to blame but himself since he had accepted her unhappiness, desperation, and need as though it were a gift of love. Did such as that often pass for love? If it did, then it was bound to make a strange sort of glue that could only survive the bad times but not the good. Great God, but he was drunk. The whiskey filled him with heat; he exhaled it like the breath of a furnace; it bathed the back of his eyes, the good one as well as the bad; and he was afraid to move. But he knew what he knew. He had become a sad old man who could only wait around until the next disaster reduced her to the sort of needs that he could satisfy. And how long would it be before he wished for some catastrophe to overtake her? Who was to say he didn't already? Carefully and with as much dignity as he could muster, he reached for a can of beer, but the whiskey he had drunk seemed to jostle him like a ride on a city bus and he nearly fell.

He was still carefully propped on his stool when the party broke up at quarter of three in the morning, and he waved good-bye to everyone from there. But Sally Ann was full of life. As rosy and glowing as a gemstone they had polished, she saw them off down the sidewalk.

"They like me," she told him when she came back inside the littered apartment. "I think they actually like me."

"Soooorly," he said. He licked his lips to loosen them up, but they felt as insensitive and ungainly as tractor tires. "Ssshhooer," he said. If a fellow didn't speak a word all evening, it was clear he could forget just how it was done.

She gave him a sharp, appraising glance. "Gee," she said,

"you sure managed to get shit-faced."

Holding a sweating can of beer snuggled against his chest where it dampened his shirtfront, he rubbed his face awkwardly with his free hand in order to loosen up his lips, but she went off into the kitchen before he could speak. By the time she was back with a plastic bag, collecting beer cans and dumping ashtrays, he had forgotten what he wished to say.

"They think I can do it," she said, but whether to him or herself he wasn't sure. "They think I can study anything I want."

Oh, but she was flushed and glowing and very lovely, and he realized that somehow, in spite of everything that had happened to her in her life, she had remained mysteriously unmarked. Of course her new friends liked her. How could they not? She had spirit and heart and the endearing capacity to make the same mistakes over and over. There was something incorruptible and therefore unteachable about her.

She stopped directly in front of him and looked him in the eye. "They think I can be an artist or a businesswoman or a lawyer or anything, and just maybe I can. So," she said, "what do you have to say on the subject?"

Wisdom was one thing, honesty another. He'd never had any talent at all for telling a woman something that would hurt her; it seemed almost as unthinkable as hitting her with his fist. He nodded his head.

"You don't think it's too late?"

He wagged his head from side to side, and although there was nothing the least extravagant in the gesture, it made the room spin violently, nearly pitching him off his stool. For a moment he thought of claiming the privilege of a drunk and slipping bonelessly to the floor, where he could pretend to be unconscious.

"Oh, Toots," she said, "how am I supposed to know what to do or who to be?"

His great wisdom aside, he could not help her. Anyway,

he could feel all powers of discrimination slipping away from him, as the power of speech and locomotion had already done. Her face, as full of light as a stained glass window, drew very close to his. "What," she said, "are you just going to sit on that damned stool all night?"

"Yesh," he whispered.

Somehow he must have achieved a perfect distribution of weight and balance, and apparently he hadn't moved once during the night, since, when he woke a little after eight the next day, his butt felt welded to the seat of the stool, and the muscles of his neck and the small of his back had seized as though with rigor mortis. For a long moment he didn't think he'd ever be able to move again. He couldn't even seem to lift the back of his neck from the wall until he raised a hand, got a grip on his hair, and pulled his head forward. He sat for a moment, holding his head in his hands while the small of his back and his neck greeted this new posture with outrageous layers of pain. He had never felt worse. His good eye felt screwed into its socket. His brain was sore. And he was sick to his stomach.

When he discovered he was still holding the last can of beer he'd opened pressed unconsciously into one cheek, carefully, cradling the back of his neck with one hand, he tilted his head back and drank it. While his stomach worked to make peace with the warm, flat beer, he tried to gather the courage to stand, and as he did, he found that he was not only hung over, but still a little drunk. No matter, he thought, and made his way carefully into the kitchen where he cracked two raw eggs into a glass and, getting a grip on the back of his neck again, drank them too.

In the bathroom down the hall, he shed the eyepatch, dug the nose plug out of its little divot of pain, and took a handful of aspirin and a long hot shower. She was just emerging from their dim bedroom when he came out into the hall again, the gray and copper stubble gleaming on his face and a Band-Aid across his empty eye socket. "Good morning," he told her.

"Jesus," she said, her eyes puffed nearly shut with sleep, "it walks and talks."

It took him only a few moments to dress and not very much longer to pack. One of the red plaid suitcases they had bought at the bus station in Clifton was more than adequate. By the time he finished, he thought his stomach might be able to hang on to a cup of coffee, and he went off into the kitchen to make some. And while the coffeepot growled and hissed on the counter, he tried his best to compose what he would say to her, but wrapped in her terrycloth robe and still damp from her shower, she padded into the kitchen before a single phrase came to mind. Mechanically she got down cups and turned to say something to him, but whatever it was didn't come out, for all at once she caught sight of the suitcase just inside the living room door and then she searched his face, and he knew at least he would not have to tell her he was leaving. Her eyes were instantly full of the knowledge.

"Oh, Toots," she said, looking suddenly small and pale.

"You see," he told her, "it's just that I am, by nature, a solitary man."

"Oh, Toots," she said.

"It's just that people, especially women, always seem to take me by surprise."

"I'm really sorry," she said. "Honest, I didn't mean . . ."

"It's only that I can't ever seem to tell what my responsibilities are, you see, and sooner or later I'm bound to act a fool."

"You don't need to go far, do you? Maybe just across town. And money," she said. "You'll need money, and I've got bunches of that. Oh, Toots, where are you going to go?"

He had yesterday's paycheck in his pocket and he meant to tell her about it, but suddenly he began to feel very bad again. The coffeepot's incessant commotion had ceased, but not before it had filled the room with its bitter aroma. He didn't need any coffee after all, he realized. There was really only one thing he needed. "I guess I'll go to Canada," he said, watching her carefully. She was getting ready to close the space between them and put her arms around him. He could see it in her eyes. "Or maybe Alaska."

# 22

Although he was hostile and angry because Toots had disappeared without warning, Hobb agreed to buy his fish again. His profits had been off more than a third in the months Toots had been away, after all; and the only practical thing to do was to forget his anger, clean his tanks, fix his pump, and buy a full month of ads in the *Clifton Democrat.*

And all things considered, the camp was not in bad shape. Toots half-expected to find himself poking through charred rubble—a scorched and gutted mattress here, a battered kerosene lantern there, a coffee can full of nails steeping in a cankerous soup of rain water. He half-expected to live in his cave above the sweet, creosotey stench of fire and ruin. But a little work put most things right. He patched the roof, cleaned and polished the rusty cook stove, got it back on its island of tin, and even outfitted it with brand-new stovepipe. There hadn't been much damage and very little pilfering. Two of his boats and all of the catfish in his holding pool had been taken, but nothing else seemed to be missing, at least nothing he wished to call by name. Even the money he'd stashed carelessly in the Maxwell House coffee cans was still exactly where he'd left it. All he had to do, it seemed to him, was get back the proper nature and disposition. But that was exactly the quality he found most elusive.

For a very long time, no matter what he set his hand to, he felt he ought to be doing something else, and no matter where he was on the river or about the camp, it seemed to him he should be in another place. Once, when he was pulling a minnow trap in the mouth of Bear Creek, he suddenly felt so wildly alone that his hands began to shake, and he could neither open the trap nor the top of his minnow bucket. And sometimes extremely peculiar thoughts came over him without warning. Once, toward the end of November, he was running a trotline below his camp when it occurred to him that if he knew for certain no young girl in a blue dress was hiding nearby, then everything he did was without purpose, and the world itself was utterly desolate.

But he kept rigidly to himself, trapped and seined his minnows, ran his lines, and settled into a routine even more private and eccentric than ever before. He let his hair and beard grow, seldom spoke a word to anyone, seldom bathed, and would often appear to sell his fish and buy his supplies in such a state of disrepair that his old friends at the Riverside Market, and even Hobb himself, took to watching him out of the tails of their eyes, sucking their teeth and shaking their heads with condescension and pity. Twigs and leaves and unidentifiable debris in his hair and beard, his fly half-unzipped, scorifications of ancient dirt on his red, chapped hands, he might, from time to time, wander into the beer joint side of the market to have a glass of beer; but he would speak to no one. And though his good eye was still a piercing blue, it never quite rested on anything, whether man or beast, with any cognition.

Even the machinery of his body began to break down. His hands ached constantly, not merely in the cold, and from time to time, he might stop making up a trotline to consider how crooked, knobby, and stubborn his fingers had grown. On the rare occasions when they were bare, he might ponder his feet, amazed at how, all at once, his toes had rolled over on their sides. Sometimes a shoulder or knee joint would betray him, or a perfectly good tooth would grow unaccountably loose, no matter that he rubbed his gums vigorously with salt and soda. But a little at a time, sweet solitude began to visit him again. Oh but she was jealous, was solitude, and wouldn't come near if any thought of Sally Ann was in his head, and would withdraw if one of her aspects caused him to think, however fleetingly, of her rival. But by the time the first chilling winter had passed and there were silver sprays of catkins in the March willows, she kept his company. After all, she demanded only that he be faithful and not one thing more.

# Afterword

The novel I envision when I begin to write and the novel I ultimately produce inevitably bear only a slight family resemblance. But I intended *Toots in Solitude* to go differently. Disheartened with the predominantly nice, and occasionally glowing, reviews of my first three novels, which had left me as stubbornly poor as I'd been before they were written, I intended *Toots in Solitude* to be a potboiler. With malice aforethought and a considerable burden of shame, I set about to write something facile and quick that might help me get my children through college before I went back to my dogged and possibly doomed obsession with what I considered real, hardball fiction.

No rethinking and rewriting was to be my first rule, since my first three books had taken me three, five, and seven years to produce, and I would have easily made more money if I had spent my writing time pumping gas for minimum wage. *Toots* was written when I was in my middle forties, and I often spoke of it as my male menopausal novel, written about—as well as by—a man deeply afflicted with that unfortunate, often ludicrous condition. Therefore, I didn't have to research the condition of my main character; I knew him intimately, down to his last frailty and fantasy. I had in mind a lighthearted and perhaps even an outright funny little tale. All I needed, I figured, was an interesting sequence of action and a strong element of suspense.

Of course, I didn't really know how to write a potboiler and still don't. It would be nice to be that clever, but few writers I've ever met are. I suspect most of us write the best novels we are capable of writing; and if these documents catch the fancy of the reading public, all the better; and if not, more's the pity. For all my intentions, *Toots,* too, was probably the very best I could do. I wrote and rewrote over and over my one or two pages a day, and then put them aside. Yet I did keep to my original plan in one significant way: I did not rethink the design of the novel or do large, far-reaching rewrites, and so managed to resist the siren call of vastly different possibilities. In my other books this constant pausing to rethink the whole design and proportion of my story had often caused major characters to disappear altogether and minor ones to matriculate into much more significant roles. Financial pressure, I suspect, kept me from this obsessive tendency, and I finished this small document in a little over a year.

Finally, I suppose the pot didn't exactly boil, but it did simmer nicely in this country, in England, and even in Sweden, of all places. Movie options and other interests considered, *Toots* made considerably more money than my first three novels put together. Still, I'm not at all sure what appropriate and logical lessons can be learned from its relative success, since, like my others, it was not truly the book I intended.

Almost by accident it laid out for me some funny, some perhaps poignant, and some utterly horrible dynamics that can take place between men and women. But, of course, it isn't ultimately fair for a writer to claim innocence and pretend that things in his fiction happen by accident. Each book has a logic of its own, an itinerary, which may even run athwart the grade of what its author thinks he's up to. So that, at last, what I had hoped would be a rather lighthearted book became something else again. Even Solitude, which I thought I utterly craved when I began this little tale, betrayed me in the end with its unimagined dimensions.

John Yount
*Newmarket, New Hampshire*
1995

# About the Author

Author of four other critically acclaimed novels—*Wolf at the Door, The Trapper's Last Shot, Hardcastle* (reissued by SMU Press in 1992), and *Thief of Dreams* (reissued by SMU Press in 1994)—JOHN YOUNT teaches at the University of New Hampshire. He has been the recipient of a Rockefeller Grant, a Guggenheim Fellowship, and an NEA grant. He lives in New Hampshire with his wife, Deborah Navas, also a writer.

**Also from Southern Methodist University Press**

**Hardcastle**
*A Novel by* John Yount

"From now on, there are bound to be two classics of the Great Depression—*The Grapes of Wrath* and *Hardcastle.*"
—*Los Angeles Times*

"This is a strong, spare novel about love, courage and human responsibility in coal-mining Switch County, Kentucky, during the 1930s. . . . Yount takes some deep soundings of American strengths and values."—*Publishers Weekly*
ISBN 0-87074-341-4, paper

**Thief of Dreams**
*A Novel by* John Yount

Yount plumbs the pain of Madeline and Edward Tally's unhappy marriage and the resulting confusion of 13-year-old James, their only son.

"This is a wonderful story—gentle and tough, funny and sad. . . . Yount has done something brilliant: created a young boy whose actions with his family, his friend, and most importantly, alone, reveal to him enough truths for a lifetime. I haven't read so happily of such a boy since Faulkner's Ike McCaslin."—Andre Dubus
ISBN 0-87074-375-9, paper